I0534159

NAKED CITY

Every Secret Has an Address

B. S. DARA

Naked City

B. S. DARA

Naked City

© 2025 B. S. Dara

All rights reserved. No part of this book may be reproduced, stored in a retrieval system, or transmitted in any form or by any means, electronic, mechanical, photocopying, recording, or otherwise, without the prior written permission of the publisher, except in the case of brief quotations used in reviews, articles, or critical essays.

This is a work of fiction. Names, characters, places, and incidents are either products of the author's imagination or are used fictitiously. Any resemblance to actual events, locales, or people, living or dead, is entirely coincidental.

Published by *The Good Earth Publishers*

First Edition, 2025

ISBN: 979-8-9930799-0-5

Printed in the United States and India by Amazon KDP

For those who know desire keeps receipts.

Prologue

The city does not sleep; it only pretends. Behind the neon and the rain, there are always eyes open, recording, filing, saving what should have vanished into darkness.

That night was no different.

The rain had been steady since evening, turning Mumbai into a smear of lights and reflections. Windows fogged, gutters overflowed, and on every balcony the water collected in shallow pools, mirrors waiting to catch the careless. From high above, the city looked like a circuit board on the verge of burning out.

He—Subject M—moved through it quietly. Nothing distinguished him from the thousands of others ducking under plastic awnings or fighting for rickshaws. But he was marked, whether he knew it or not. Every step filed, every pause noted.

She—Subject F—entered the frame later. Different street, different pace. Her jacket clung to her shoulders, her lip carried that faint scar, a signature written into her skin. She looked like another soaked commuter, another silhouette dissolving into the crowd. But the lens never lies. She was already being catalogued, line by line.

[Observation Report | Pre-Contact]
Location: South Mumbai, scattered bars and eateries.
Time: 23:47 hrs.
Subject M: Male, ~30–32 yrs. Unremarkable clothing, solitary movement.
Subject F: Female, ~28–30 yrs. Scar on lip, movements deliberate.
Status: Convergence imminent.

The city below kept moving, hawkers folding their stalls, buses coughing black smoke, late-night chai stalls hissing with steam. No one noticed two people being mapped against each other, like coordinates closing in.

Intimacy begins long before touch. Sometimes it begins here, in the quiet record of arrivals and exits, in the timestamps no one erases.

They did not know they were being watched. They never do at the beginning. But files open. Logs start. A single note is entered, as routine as breathing:

"Subjects in motion. Contact expected within one hour. Surveillance continues."

Outside, the rain thickened. Inside the circuits of the city, two names had just been written down for the first time.

And once entered, nothing is ever erased.

1

The Match (00:07 hrs)

The rain had not stopped all day. By midnight, it had lost its urgency, falling instead with a slow persistence, like a tired hand knocking at the same locked door. Mumbai looked blurred at the edges, its outlines smudged under the weight of water. Headlights became pale streaks, neon signs ran like paint on wet canvas, and even the sea, usually restless, seemed subdued, a black mirror rippling with exhaustion.

On Chapel Road, the bar glowed like a fever that refused to break. Its sign sputtered in half-lit letters, the red flicker of *Alehouse* glowing and dimming with an electric cough. Inside, it smelled of damp leather, fried snacks, and old perfume. The bar was a place where strangers pretended they weren't, and regulars pretended not to be seen.

He was already there. A man in his early thirties, face angled toward a sweating bottle of beer he had stopped drinking. He had been sitting at the counter since half past eleven, running a finger around the rim of the glass as if trying to coax music from it. The bartender had clocked him as the quiet type, the ones who drink not for pleasure but for delay. He wasn't waiting for anyone, not really. Or maybe he was, though he didn't know it yet.

She entered at 12:07 a.m. No umbrella, no rush to shake herself dry. She stepped into the room the way someone steps into a photograph already in progress. A soaked jacket clung to her shoulders, her hair still dripping, strands dark and heavy against the pale curve of her neck. Her face was bare of make-up, but her lips carried a thin scar that caught the neon and glinted silver, like a secret that refused to stay hidden.

She ordered whiskey, neat. Her voice was low, deliberate, unhurried. The bartender poured without question but glanced at her twice. She didn't look around at first, only traced the rim of her glass with one finger, as though measuring its circumference.

He watched her. Tried not to, failed. Their eyes caught, their glance lingered half a second too long, long enough to move from accident to invitation.

[Watcher's Notes]

Location: Chapel Road bar.
Time: 00:07 hrs.
Subject F: female, estimated 28-30.
Distinguishing mark: scar on lower lip
(vertical, ~1.5 cm).
Subject M: male, estimated 30-32. Present
since 23:34 hrs. One beer (unfinished).
Contact initiated: visual. Duration: 2.3
seconds.
Observation: Mutual interest confirmed.
Neither party aware of surveillance.

Back at the counter, she lifted the glass, let the amber liquid catch the restless light, and took a slow sip. He leaned forward just enough for his words to bridge the gap between them.

"First time here?"

Her head tilted. The smile was not a smile, more a curved blade wrapped in charm. "Do you ask that to everyone who looks lost?"

He caught the sting, but it didn't wound. There was something in her tone, not cruel, not kind, but honest in its indifference.

"Only the ones who pretend they aren't," he said.

For a second the bar stilled. The jukebox murmured on, glasses clinked, laughter rose and fell at the far end, but here at the counter, silence seemed to stretch like fabric pulled too tight. She set her glass down gently, leaned her chin on her hand, and studied him as if calculating his edges.

"So which one are you?"

He raised his bottle, tilted it her way, and drank. It was a non-answer, but it was also the only answer worth giving.

The rain outside thickened, a steady percussion against the door. She shifted to the stool beside him without asking, her arm brushing his. The contact was casual, deliberate.

"Men drinks to think," she said.

"And women drink to forget."

She raised an eyebrow. "What makes you so sure?"

"Because you ordered whiskey neat."

Her laugh was quiet, more exhale than sound. It curled between them like smoke. She drank again, and he watched the glass touch her scar before meeting her lips.

They spoke the way strangers do when they're both a little reckless, names exchanged without surnames, jobs described without details, truths confessed in half-shadows. He told her he worked in "finance" but left out that he was drowning in debt. She said she was in "marketing" but skipped the part about the boss she was sleeping with. The lies were easy, the omissions easier.

Outside, the rain drummed. Inside, something quickened.

When the clock ticked past one, she closed her tab, sliding notes onto the counter with a hand that didn't tremble. He stood too, more instinct than decision.

"Going somewhere?" he asked.

"Home." She didn't add *alone.*

The bar had thinned. The students were gone, the jukebox silenced. Rain hissed louder when the door opened. They stepped into it together, their bodies haloed briefly by neon before the night swallowed them whole.

They walked without speaking, the rain filling the silence. Taxi drivers slowed but weren't hailed. He glanced at her, wondering if she would vanish into the wet dark with a casual wave, but she stayed close, her stride aligned with his.

At the corner, under a streetlamp haloed with water, she turned to him.

"Your place or mine?"

The city was a bruise of light and shadow around them. He opened his mouth to answer, but in truth, the choice had already been made long before.

2

The Apartment

His apartment was small, one-bedroom that wore its compromises on the walls. The white paint had yellowed near the ceiling fan, the tube-light flickered when he switched it on, and the window looked out onto another building so close you could almost touch it. But to her, it was a refuge, anonymous, ordinary, and safe enough for what it needed to be tonight.

They entered together without speaking. He dropped his keys into a chipped bowl by the door. She slipped her jacket off and draped it across a chair, not asking where. There was a silence, heavy but not awkward, filled by the faint sounds of Mumbai bleeding through the walls: a watchman's whistle somewhere below.

He opened the fridge and found a lone beer, warm from neglect. "It's not cold," he said.

"I didn't come for that," she replied.

It was a line delivered without emphasis. He closed the fridge and turned. She was leaning against the wall, arms folded, eyes steady. The scar on her lip caught the light again, silver against the dull tube-light.

They moved toward each other as if drawn by a force older than intention. Two strangers who had carried their silence long enough to want them broken.

He thought of how quickly it had happened, an hour ago he'd been tracing condensation on a beer bottle, now she was in his apartment. The acceleration thrilled him, but beneath the thrill was a faint terror: nothing that arrived this fast ever stayed.

She thought of how ordinary his apartment was. The bed was unmade, the curtains plain, a stack of unpaid bills on the table. She catalogued the details the way some people memorize exits: mental notes, escape routes. She had slept in better rooms, worse rooms, but none that felt more temporary than this.

They undressed with the kind of efficiency that pretends at passion. Clothes fell without drama. Their bodies found each other, but even in closeness there was distance, a faint self-consciousness that shadowed every movement.

He kissed her and she let him, not resisting, not surrendering, merely allowing. Her thoughts wandered, to the scar, to the bills on his table, to the possibility that he was lying about everything. She didn't care, not tonight.

For him, desire came tangled with fear, fear of saying too much, of asking, of revealing the debt that sat like a stone in his chest. So he stayed quiet, channeling his truths into touch instead of words.

Location: Subject M's residence.
Time: 02:03 hrs.
Both subjects present.
Observation: Physical intimacy initiated.
Lights left on. Curtains drawn.
Surveillance continues.

Later, when the urgency subsided, they lay on the bed in silence. The sheets smelled faintly of detergent and dampness. He watched the ceiling fan spin, listening to the faint tick in its motor. She traced circles on her own arm, her mind elsewhere.

"You don't talk much," she said finally.

"You don't ask much," he countered.

She smiled faintly. "Maybe that's why we're here."

It wasn't affection, not yet. Two people aware they weren't building anything permanent, only colliding in the present.

He wanted to ask about her scar. He didn't. She wanted to ask why he looked like he hadn't slept in days. She didn't. Both had questions, both carried secrets, and both knew better than to demand answers too soon.

She rose first, padding barefoot to the bathroom. The light spilled under the door, a square of brightness on the floor. He lay back, eyes half-shut, listening to the tap run, then stop. She returned, pulled the sheet around herself, and sat by the window.

"You live here alone?" she asked.

"Yes."

"Good."

He didn't ask what she meant.

The city outside was restless. Even at two-thirty in the morning, there were horns in the distance, sound of scooter engines and dogs barking. Mumbai never went silent, not fully. She liked that. Silence was dangerous; it left too much space for thought. Noise was a shield.

She smoked one of his cigarettes without asking, exhaling into the humid night. He watched her silhouette, the red tip glowing with each drag. She looked like a photograph he would never be able to explain.

He thought of his debts, the messages he had ignored, the collectors who would not stay ignored for long. She thought of her office, of the text messages she had left unread, of the man whose name she refused to say aloud. Neither confessed.

By the time sleep reached them, it wasn't shared. They lay beside each other, but their dreams were separate, their bodies aligned but their thoughts running parallel like trains on different tracks.

Time: 03:46 hrs.
Subjects remained at same location
overnight.
Observation: No external interruptions.
Status: Stable. Recording continues.

Dawn seeped into the apartment through thin curtains. The city below stirred awake, newspaper bundles thudding onto pavements, milk packets clinking in plastic crates. She woke first, watching the light shift on the wall. He stirred after, blinking against the brightness.

Neither spoke of what had happened. What bound them wasn't tenderness. They weren't falling in love. They were colliding. And somewhere beyond the walls, someone was watching

3

The Password Exchange

His flat had not been meant for two. The kitchen was barely the width of one outstretched arm, the sofa sagged in the middle, and the bathroom door refused to close without a push. Yet by the third morning, her toothbrush leaned against his in a chipped mug, a pair of her slippers sat near the bed, and his shirts carried the faint perfume of someone who hadn't been there a week ago.

It should have felt temporary, like a guest overstaying, but it didn't. It felt invasive in a way that was oddly comforting, as though he had been waiting for this quiet disruption.

She brewed tea that morning as though she had always known where the strainer was kept. He watched from the doorway, half-amused, half-uneasy.

"You're out of sugar," she said.

"I don't take sugar."

"Now you do," she replied, tipping half a spoon into his cup. He didn't argue.

They drank in silence. Outside, a fruit vendor called out his prices. Life carried on, unbothered by how fast two strangers had become a unit.

The flat seemed to watch them. The unwashed cups, the bills on the table, the walls that had absorbed his loneliness for months, everything sat quietly, as though relieved to have its silence broken.

Later, stretched across his bed with the curtain drawn against the day, she scrolled through her phone. A message arrived, the screen flashing bright, and she turned it toward him.

"Here," she said. "Hold this."

He frowned. "What am I holding?"

"My life," she answered, almost lightly, and rattled off her unlock code before passing the phone to him. He entered it, saw the home screen open, chats, photos, emails, bank app icons lined up like temptations. He didn't touch anything, but the trust startled him.

It wasn't trust. It was a dare.

An hour later, when he left his own phone on the table to shower, she glanced at it, tapped the screen, and waited. The lock pattern glowed faintly, smudged by his own fingerprints. She traced it without hesitation. The phone opened. She didn't look deeper, not yet. She only wanted to know that she could.

They began to swap details in small increments, like smugglers trading contraband: a PIN here, a password there. A borrowed debit card, a shared ride-hailing account, a half-finished email left open. It was intimacy by transparency, but the transparency came too easily, like glass that cracks under the lightest pressure.

At a café in Bandra the next evening, they sat across from each other with laptops open, working as though they had always worked side by side. She leaned over, typed her Wi-Fi password on his screen. He tilted his device toward her, letting her copy his Netflix login. To the waiters, to the other customers, they looked like an old couple in sync.

To him, it felt like love disguised as efficiency. To her, it felt like efficiency disguised as love.

[Watcher's Notes]

Timeline: 72 hours since first contact.
Data exchange initiated.
Subject F provided phone passcode (4 digits). Subject M reciprocated (pattern unlock).
Shared accounts observed: transport, entertainment, banking (partial).
Assessment: Boundaries collapsed at abnormal speed. Monitoring continues.

That night, she stayed again. They lay side by side on the bed, scrolling through each other's photos. He showed her childhood snapshots his mother had sent. She showed him old vacation pictures, cropped carefully to remove a figure he didn't ask about.

"Delete this one," she said suddenly, pointing to an image of her at a beach.

"Why?"

"I don't like how I look."

He pressed the delete icon without hesitation, though he suspected the reason had little to do with vanity.

It was too soon for this closeness, too reckless. But in the half-light, neither of them slowed.

In the following days, their lives folded into each other like clothes stuffed into the same drawer. She answered his phone once when a number flashed unfamiliar. He used her laptop without asking. They bought groceries together, and fell asleep on the sofa with the TV still humming.

It was not love, not yet. But it had the shape of it, the convenience of it, the rhythm of it. They had skipped the slow work of discovery and jumped straight to familiarity, as if intimacy were a password you only had to type once to gain entry.

And yet, beneath the ease, shadows collected. He wondered if her laughter came too easily, if it was a cover for something darker. She wondered if his silences were patience or concealment. They never asked. They only handed each other more keys, more codes, more ways in.

The relationship has gone from strangers, co-habiting rhythm in *three days*.

By the end of the week, her toothbrush wasn't the only thing standing in his flat. A spare set of clothes hung in his wardrobe, her perfume lingered in the bathroom, and her presence had imprinted itself on the walls. It looked, to anyone else, like the beginning of a life shared.

But beginnings built this fast never last long.

4

Someone Watching

The mornings had begun to look different. Not brighter, not softer, just different. She woke before him, always. Sat by the window with a cigarette or her phone, half-draped in the sheet, letting the city filter into her before he did. He liked to pretend he was still asleep, watching her silhouette framed by the thin curtains, the red tip of her cigarette flaring against the grey light.

This morning, though, something shifted. She froze halfway through a drag, eyes narrowing. He followed her gaze and saw nothing at first, just the opposite building with its balconies and drying clothes. Then he saw it, a figure behind a rusted grille, still as furniture, staring across.

When she noticed he was awake, she exhaled, almost amused. "Your neighbor should charge rent for the way he looks at us."

He pushed himself up on one elbow, blinked against the light. The figure was gone. A curtain swayed where it had been.

"Which one?" he asked.

"Doesn't matter. He saw enough." She stubbed her cigarette, let the ash fall in the chipped mug on the sill. "Let him look."

She said it like a dare, but he caught the faint shadow under her voice.

The day unfolded like every other since they had folded into each other's lives. He left for work later than usual, distracted by the echo of her words. At his office, the emails piled up, deadlines blinked red on his screen. He stared at them without really reading. When his phone buzzed with a new notification, he frowned.

Location Services Enabled: You were at Chapel Road Alehouse. Share with friends?

He didn't remember turning that on. He swiped it away, irritation tightening his jaw. His debt collector had called twice already that morning. He muted the phone, shoving it into his drawer.

At her office, she was less lucky. A message blinked on her laptop: *Unusual sign-in attempt detected.* It was her personal account. She changed the password quickly, glanced around the open-plan room. Everyone else was typing, drinking coffee, scrolling through presentations. None of them looked up. She kept her expression flat, even when her hands trembled slightly on the keyboard.

She thought of the phone she had unlocked for him the night before. How easily the numbers had slipped from her lips. Four digits, no hesitation. She thought of his pattern unlock, the smudge marks on his screen. Too easy.

They met for dinner in Bandra, at a small place with checked tablecloths and fans that only moved the heat around. She told him about the email, keeping her voice light, as though it were only a glitch. He told her about the notification, shrugged as if it were nothing. They both laughed it off, almost convincingly.

But when she reached across the table for his glass, her hand lingered on his wrist longer than it needed to. When he paid the bill in cash instead of card, she noticed.

On the walk back, they took the longer route through quieter lanes. A stray dog trailed them for a while, then veered off. He slipped his hand into hers, tentative. She let it stay there, though her eyes kept flicking to the reflections in the shop windows, half-expecting to catch someone too close behind them.

At the building, the lift was crowded with neighbours. A woman with a child balanced on her hip, a man with a grocery bag dripping water. As the doors slid open at their floor, the man gave a small smile.

"Nice to see young people these days settling in together so fast," he said, stepping aside to let them pass.

They both froze for half a second too long before forcing polite smiles. Once the door of the flat closed behind them, she laughed, sharp and humorless.

"Settling in? We've barely met."

He tried to joke it away, but the words felt brittle.

[Watcher's Notes]

[09:14 hrs | Opposite building, Chapel Road]

Subject F observed at window. Duration: 47 seconds.

That night, the flat carried their unease like smoke. They moved around each other carefully, brushing teeth, changing clothes, lying down. He kept the curtains drawn this time. She kept her phone under the pillow.

In the darkness, he whispered, "Do you think someone's...."

"Yes," she said, cutting him off

The fan ticked above them, louder than usual. The city noise outside seemed too sharp, every horn, every bark, every shout amplified.

They didn't touch that night. Sleep came late, broken, crowded with the sense of eyes pressing against the walls

5

The Lie of Normalcy

By the weekend, they had learned how to act like a couple in public. It wasn't rehearsed, but it carried the smoothness of a play they both knew the lines to. Brunches, shared rickshaws, her hand slipping into his as if it had always belonged there.

On Sunday morning they sat in a café in Bandra, sunlight pouring across the cracked wooden tables. She ordered pancakes, he ordered black coffee, and they argued half-seriously over whether to split the bill. The couple at the next table leaned toward each other, laughing. She tilted her head, imitated the gesture, and for a second, he felt the strange ache of déjà vu, as if they were borrowing someone else's intimacy.

He watched her stir syrup into her coffee, eyes glinting. She knew she was being watched, not just by him, but by the room, and she played to it. Crossing her legs just so, smiling at his jokes with perfect timing. The performance was seamless.

"See?" she whispered, leaning closer. "We look normal."

"Maybe we are," he replied.

Neither believed it.

At her office, she made a show of returning to routine. Meetings, emails, PowerPoint decks that blurred into one another. Colleagues asked about her weekend, and she laughed lightly, said it was good. She didn't mention the flat, the toothbrush, the passwords. The omission tasted sweet, like hiding a bruise under silk.

He did the same. In his office, he kept his voice casual, his gestures calm. When his colleague noticed the faint mark of ash on his cuff, he said he'd been smoking on the balcony. He didn't mention her cigarettes, her laugh in his kitchen, the way her perfume had taken up residence on his sheets.

The lie of normalcy was easier than honesty. Normalcy was what people expected. Normalcy was invisible.

At night, they carried that lie into the flat. Groceries on the table, Netflix humming in the background, arguments about what to order for dinner. The routine rituals unfolded, but their edges were too sharp. He noticed her phone turned screen-side down more often. She noticed his calls were taken in the stairwell.

They didn't speak of it. They only leaned harder into the performance, as though acting would make it real.

One evening, they went to dinner with her colleagues. He sat through stories about campaigns and deadlines, nodded at names he didn't recognize. She brushed her hand against his under the table, smiled at him in ways designed for others to notice.

21

"You're lucky," one of her coworkers said to him, tipsy on wine. "She's a catch."

He smiled, though the word *lucky* felt foreign. Later, when they left the restaurant, she laughed into the night air, but it sounded hollow.

[Watcher's Notes]

[20:46 hrs | Bandra café]

Subjects observed together.
Public behavior consistent with couple status.
Duration: 57 minutes.

The flat grew heavier with each passing day. They filled it with chatter, with sex, with food delivery bags, but silence always returned like a tide. Sometimes she caught him staring too long at her scar. Sometimes he caught her scrolling too long on old messages she claimed were work.

One night, while he cooked noodles in the cramped kitchen, she leaned in the doorway and said, "Do you think this is real?"

He didn't look up from the pot. "What?"

"This. Us."

The noodles hissed as he stirred. "Does it matter?"

She didn't answer. She walked to the window instead, lit a cigarette, and stared at the opposite building. Curtains moved.

They kept building their normalcy like scaffolding, piece by piece. Grocery lists, laundry cycles, shared alarm clocks. On the surface, it looked sturdy. Inside, it groaned under the weight of lies.

Neither did they admitted how much they depended on it. Neither admitted how fragile it was.

6

The First Crack (Thursday)

Once, in her first job, she had been called into the boss's office. He wanted an alibi, not a report. She had lied without blinking, said he had been at the office when he hadn't. A simple sentence that saved his contract and tied her fate to his.

Later, she realized he had chosen her because he knew she would do it.

That day she discovered that silence was expensive but lies were currency. And she had been trading ever since.

It was a Thursday when she didn't come back.

He had waited, first casually, then tensely, then angrily, watching the clock slip toward midnight. The flat felt smaller with every passing hour. Her cigarette pack was on the table, her slippers by the bed, but the space where she should have been stretched wide, hollow.

By one a.m. he opened the fridge, drank straight from a bottle of water, then sat at the edge of the bed with the light off. He told himself she was working late, maybe with colleagues, maybe at some client dinner. But he knew better. She didn't leave her phone on silent. She didn't vanish without a word.

When she walked in at dawn, he was still awake.

Her hair smelled faintly of rain and smoke, her jacket carried someone else's cologne. She didn't look surprised to see him sitting there.

"You waited up?" she asked, voice neutral.

"You didn't call."

"I was at work."

"All night?"

She slipped past him into the bathroom, shutting the door before he could answer himself.

The day after, he tried to play it normal. Coffee, shower, work shirts. She moved around the flat like nothing had shifted, as though the crack wasn't visible. She hummed while making tea. She brushed ash into the sink with her finger. She asked if he wanted eggs.

But he noticed the faint redness on her wrist, a mark not made by him. He noticed the way her eyes avoided his when she spoke. He noticed that her phone was now face-down, charging by the bed.

At his office, he couldn't focus. His debts pressed harder that day, collectors calling, threats tucked behind polite words. He shut his phone off, but silence didn't help. He opened his laptop and stared at spreadsheets that blurred into nonsense.

He thought of her jacket smelling of cologne. He thought of her walking in without apology. He thought of how quickly she had slipped into his life, how quickly she might slip out.

By lunch, his chest ached with something sour. It was not heartbreak, not yet, but suspicion curdled into anger.

That evening, she was already home when he returned. Cooking noodles, humming again, as though sound could erase the rising agitation inside his chest. She smiled faintly when he entered, handed him a plate.

"You're early."

"You're not," he said.

She blinked at him, then kept stirring the pot. "I told you. I was at work."

"All night?"

"Campaign deadlines. It happens."

He ate in silence, watching her chew without meeting his eyes.

[Watcher's Notes]

[05:32 hrs | Subject M's residence]

Subject F reentered after prolonged absence.
Duration away: 6 hrs 17 mins unaccounted.
Explanation: unverifiable.

26

Later, in bed, he reached for her. She let him, her body warm, her breath steady, but her mind somewhere else. He could feel the distance even with their skin touching. He stopped halfway, rolled away, stared at the ceiling fan ticking out seconds.

She whispered into the dark, "You don't trust me."

"Should I?"

She didn't answer. Her silence was louder than words.

The crack stayed. It lived in the room with them, invisible but unmissable. In the morning, they brushed their teeth side by side without speaking. At breakfast, he poured sugar into his tea though he hated it. She didn't notice. No, she did but didn't say a word.

At work, he found himself checking his phone obsessively. Opening her messages, rereading their exchanges from days before, as if searching for clues. He noticed the times her double-ticks stayed grey longer than they should. He noticed the photos she hadn't deleted from her gallery. He noticed the way her typing dots appeared and vanished, appeared again, then nothing.

He wondered who she was talking to when she wasn't talking to him.

That night, she came home early. Kissed him on the cheek, softer than usual. She poured him a drink, sat cross-legged on the sofa, scrolling through her phone. He asked nothing. She offered nothing.

The lie of normalcy held for the outside world. Inside, the crack widened.

His Ghosts

He remembered being twelve, watching his father sign papers he couldn't read. The men at the door had smiled too much, offered tea, and left with the deed to half the house. That night his father had said nothing, just smoked until the ashtray overflowed.

He had learned then: signatures kill faster than knives.

Now, years later, every time he pressed his pen to paper, forms, receipts, bills, the memory returned. It was not the debt that scared him. It was the ink.

The calls began again on Monday.

He muted the phone the first time, pressed decline the second, let it ring the third. By the fourth, she noticed. They were sitting at the kitchen table, leftover rice between them, when the vibration rattled the surface.

"You're popular," she said, reaching for her cigarette.

"Wrong number."

The screen lit up again. *Same number.*

She raised an eyebrow. "Persistent wrong number."

He picked it up, carried it to the balcony, and answered. His voice was low, strained. She couldn't hear the words, but she heard the tone. When he came back inside, his shoulders were tense, his smile forced.

"Work," he said.

"Always is."

Two nights later, they were on Carter Road, walking past the sea. She held his hand loosely, flicking ash with the other. His phone rang again. This time she stopped walking.

"Are you going to answer it, or should I?"

He pulled his hand free, shoved the phone into his pocket. "Drop it."

She studied his face, the lines carved deeper now. "If you want me not to ask, then you should try harder not to look guilty."

He lit a cigarette of his own, dragged the smoke deep. "It's not what you think."

"Then what is it?"

"Later."

"Later never comes with you."

The next day, he found a man waiting near his building. Stocky, with a cheap shirt and polished shoes. Someone who looked like he had been hired for his presence, not his conversation.

"You're hard to catch," the man said, stepping closer. "Boss wants to know when you're paying."

"Soon."

"You said soon last week."

"I'll have it."

The man smiled without warmth. "He's patient. I'm not."

From above, she watched through the window. He didn't see her. She saw everything.

When he came upstairs, she didn't mention it. She only poured him tea and waited.

That evening, while folding laundry, she spoke without looking up. "So, who's your patient friend?"

He dropped his shirt onto the sofa. "What?"

"The one downstairs. Polished shoes. Waiting."

He froze, then forced a shrug. "Salesman."

"Salesmen don't threaten."

"You misheard."

"I wasn't close enough to hear, remember? I was watching."

He sat down heavily, rubbed his eyes. "It's nothing."

"It's never nothing."

Silence stretched until it felt like another body in the room. She lit a cigarette, leaned back, and blew smoke toward the ceiling.

"You going to tell me, or do I wait for polished shoes to come upstairs next time?"

[Watcher's Notes]

[18:22 hrs | Carter Road]

Subject M approached by male individual.
Exchange: brief, low volume.
Outcome: Subject M evasive.
Observation: Debt interaction probable.

Mumbai did not sleep. It only shifted. Day vendors gave way to night sellers; cars thinned into rickshaws, rickshaws into bicycles, bicycles into footsteps. Every hour the city shed one skin for another.

Somewhere a bar shut its lights, but a stall lit a stove. Somewhere a lover slipped home, while a stranger slid into another's bed.

If you watched long enough, you understood: Mumbai never judged. It absorbed. Spit out headlines, devoured tragedies, wore blood like monsoon stains.

Their story was not the only one. It was one of thousands pulsing beneath its smog. And by tomorrow, the city would be ready for the next.

The fight came later, sharp and fast.

"You think you can keep me here and not tell me the truth?" she snapped.

"I didn't ask you to stay," he shot back.

"No, but you wanted me to. There's a difference."

He threw his keys onto the table, the sound sharp. "It's my problem. Not yours."

"That's the point. You don't get to choose what's mine now."

He looked at her then, really looked, as if realizing she had already claimed parts of his life he hadn't offered. The toothbrush, the passwords, the slippers by his bed. She had slipped in quietly, but now she stood like a mirror he couldn't turn away from.

She stubbed out her cigarette, grabbed her jacket. "If you want me to stay, you don't lie. If you want me gone, keep going."

The door shut behind her with a final click.

He sat alone, staring at the ashtray, the half-smoked cigarette still burning. His phone buzzed again. This time he didn't pick it up.

7

The Stranger's Photograph

She returned in the afternoon, when the heat pressed against the building and the watchman had settled into his chair with a newspaper. She did not text him. She climbed the stairs with slow, even steps, a paper bag in one hand, keys in the other. The door gave with the usual sticky resistance. The flat smelled of last night's cigarette smoke and the lemon cleaner he used when he wanted to look like he had tried.

She placed the bag on the table and stood still, letting the room draw itself around her. His shirts waited on the back of a chair. A cup with a ring of tea at the bottom. She moved through the space, touching nothing, cataloguing everything.

Her phone charger was by the bed. She picked it up and slipped it into her pocket. On the bedside table a drawer sat a fraction open, not careless, not closed either. She pushed it with a fingertip, meaning only to align it with the edge. The runners gave a small sound, metal against metal. The drawer opened another inch.

Inside, a passport rested on a folded handkerchief, a packet of old receipts bound with an elastic band, a pen with blue ink that had leaked onto the cap. She should have shut it. She did not. She slid the drawer open until the wood ran gentle against its stop.

The photograph lay beneath the passport. Not a screen, not a cloud, not something that could be swiped away. A real photograph, edges softened by time, the surface faintly scarred. She lifted it with care, pinching two corners, as if the image could bruise.

He stood on the left, younger by a few years, hair longer, weight a little different. The woman stood close enough that their shoulders touched, her chin tilted to meet the camera. She wore a ring that caught the light. Behind them, a hand-painted signboard named a hotel in cursive letters, and a line of hills rose soft and blue. The light in the picture had the thin, bright quality of a place above the city, air cleaner, distance real. Maybe Mahabaleshwar or Lonavala. Somewhere that sold strawberries by the basket and sweaters when it rained.

She turned the photograph over. There, in small handwriting, was a date, two years earlier, and three words. Always, Riya.

She stood with the photograph in her hand and felt the room draw tighter, as if the walls had moved in by an inch. She could hear the watchman's whistle below, the scooter that never idled quietly, the neighbour's mixer grinding spices into a paste. The world carried on, small and loud. The picture in her hand was silent.

His footsteps sounded in the corridor before his key turned. She placed the photograph face down on the bed, slid the drawer shut, and sat in the chair by the window with her legs crossed at the ankle. When the door opened, she was reading a message that had not yet arrived.

"You are here," he said. Surprise, then a quick smile, trying to get ahead of trouble.

"I came for my charger," she said. "And tea."

He went to the kitchen and filled the kettle, his movements careful, "Do you want sugar," he asked, "or are we doing that thing again."

"Half a spoon," she said.

He brought the cups. She watched his hands. A small cut on his knuckle, a faint ink stain on his thumb. He sat across from her at the table and waited for her to set the topic, the way people do when they sense a line has been drawn and do not know on which side they are standing.

"I found a photograph," she said.

He did not glance at the drawer. He looked at her face first, as if the photograph might be written there. "Which one."

"The one with you and a woman. Hills in the background. Blue light."

He took a breath, shallow. "An old picture."

"Old is not a description," she said. "It is a distance."

He reached for his tea and did not drink. "We were engaged," he said. The words fell flat on the table, without adornment. "It did not work."

"Riya," she said. "Always, Riya."

His eyes flicked. He had not wanted her to see the back. "Yes."

"Are you married." She held his gaze, steady. She did not raise her voice. The question sat between them, heavy as a new piece of furniture.

"No," he said. "Not now."

"Not now is not no." She lifted the photograph again, held it like evidence, like a fragile thing. "Why keep it."

"Because I did not throw it away," he said. "Because some things do not leave when you tell them to."

"Or because you could not decide which story you planned to tell me," she said. "The one where she was a friend. The one where she was a mistake. The one where you are the man who is always trying."

He leaned back, eyes on the ceiling for a second, as if answers might be written there in hairline cracks. "She left," he said. "I did not."

"That is not a story," she said. "That is a posture."

He set the cup down and pushed his chair back a few inches. "You opened my drawer."

"You left it open," she said.

36

"That is not the same."

"You invited me into your phone," she said. "Into your accounts. Into your bed. Do not pretend the drawer is sacred."

He rubbed his knuckle with his thumb, the cut turning white under pressure. "We were engaged," he said again. "Her parents wanted something else. She wanted something else. It ended. I owe money. The rest you know."

"You keep the photograph because you cannot decide if you are the man who lost her, or the man who will lose everything," she said. "Maybe both."

He did not argue. He reached for the picture, and she did not hand it over. He did not insist. He stood and walked to the sink and turned the tap on and off again without filling anything. Then he returned to the table and sat with his hands folded, as if the interview had resumed.

"Are you seeing her," she asked.

"No."

"Do you still speak."

"No."

"Does she know where you live."

"No," he said. He did not look at the door when he said it. He did not look at the window. His eyes stayed on her face, as if truth were a test you passed by refusing to blink.

She placed the photograph on the table between them, face up now, the ring catching the light. She watched it as if it might alter by looking. In the picture he had an arm lifted off frame, likely around the woman's shoulder. In the room he kept his hands still, palms down, a man who knew that movement would only make things break.

"Do you want me to throw it away," he asked.

"I want you to tell me why you did not," she said.

"Because I did not think about it," he said. "Because everything else was louder. Debt. Work. You. Every day a list. Throwing away a photograph did not make the list."

"Do not put me on a list with your debt," she said, and her voice had an edge now, clean and thin.

He nodded. "You are not on a list," he said. "You are the thing that is not a list."

She almost smiled. Almost. "You are not clever," she said softly. "Not today."

His phone vibrated on the table. The number was not saved. He let it ring once, twice, three times, then turned it over. Silence returned with a small snap, as if it had broken and been repaired.

She rose and walked to the window. The opposite building stared back, balconies with shirts hung to dry, a child's bicycle leaning against a railing, a row of empty pots. Curtains shifted on the third floor. She did not look away.

He spoke without standing. "Do you want to stay."

"You want me to," she said.

"That is not the question."

She turned from the window and leaned against the sill, arms folded. "If I stay," she said, "you tell me when polished shoes come back. You tell me when you do not answer. You tell me who calls. And if there is another photograph, you do not let me find it. You hand it to me."

He held her eyes and nodded once. It was a small nod that means a person has agreed to a thing they do not know how to do.

"Who kept this photograph," she asked. "You, or the man you were with her."

"Both," he said. The honesty surprised him. It surprised her.

She picked up the picture and turned it over again. The date remained the same. The promise on the back did not fade under her thumb. She placed the photograph back into the drawer herself, sliding it under the passport, lining the edges, closing the wood until it sat flush. Then she placed the keys on top of the table where he could see them.

"I will be at my place tonight," she said. "I want to sleep where the walls do not have to remember."

He did not stop her. He did not ask for a different ending. He stood and followed her to the door and held it open, and as she crossed the threshold, she touched his arm once, light as a check for fever.

In the corridor she paused and turned back. "Tell me if she calls," she said.

"She will not," he said.

The stairwell smelled of damp concrete and paint. Below, the watchman had moved from his chair to the gate. He opened it with a scrape and a nod. The afternoon sun looked bleached and without patience. She walked past the chai stall and the woman selling flowers from a basket and the boy loading crates into a tempo, then turned into the lane that had no shade.

He stayed at the doorway until she did not look like herself any longer, only a person moving away. Then he went back to the table and sat. He picked up his phone and put it down again. He opened the drawer and looked at the clean rectangle where the photograph had been. For a second he thought she had taken it. His chest tightened. Then he slid the passport aside and saw the edge of the picture and let out a breath he had not known he was holding.

He shut the drawer and set his palm flat on the wood. The surface was warm. It felt like a pulse.

In the evening, he walked without plan, turning corners by feel. Carter Road, then a lane that always smelled of frying and diesel, then a shop that sold lottery tickets and phone covers. He bought cigarettes and did not light one. He watched couples pass, their conversations private and ordinary, and felt outside the word ordinary in a way that tightened the skin across his shoulders.

When he returned, night had slid over the building that it made the windows look like empty eyes. He turned the key and stepped into the flat with the care of a person entering a room where someone might be sleeping. The table looked as it had in the afternoon. The chair waited. The fan turned. The drawer stayed shut.

He opened his laptop and stared at the banking site. The numbers did not alter no matter how long he looked. He wrote a message to a colleague, closed it before sending, wrote a different message to a different person, closed that too. Then he stood and went to the sink and washed the two cups without needing to.

The doorbell rang just before ten. He expected her. He expected the man with polished shoes. He found neither.

A woman from two floors down stood in the corridor, a plastic container in her hand. "My maid made too much," she said. "Take."

He thanked her and took the container and watched her go. The kindness made the room feel strange, like a mirror that had been moved by an inch.

He ate standing at the counter, tasting nothing. Then he sat by the window and watched the building opposite until the lights went out one by one. He waited for the third-floor curtain to move. It did not.

He slept on the sofa without meaning to, woke with a neck that ached and a taste in his mouth like old metal. He showered and dressed and stood in the doorway with his bag over his shoulder, looking back at the table, at the drawer, at the absence of one pair of slippers by the bed. Then he locked the door and left.

[Watcher's Notes]

[16:41 hrs | Subject M's residence]
Subject F present earlier without Subject M.
Exit observed at 16:18 hrs via stairwell.
Subject M returned at 19:40 hrs.
No third party observed on corridor camera.

The next morning, she messaged him.

Tea? Seven?

He wrote *Yes*. He did not add anything else.

At seven she arrived with jasmine in her hair and the careful, guarded expression of someone who has decided to try again without saying the word try.

They drank tea in the quiet, side by side on the window ledge, two people looking at the same street and pretending it was a view. She handed him a folded slip of paper.

"What is this," he asked.

"My new password," she said. "You changed yours yet."

He shook his head. "Not yet."

"Do it," she said.

He placed the paper in his wallet without unfolding it. They finished their tea and washed the cups. She took her slippers from the corner and left them by the bed. He pretended not to notice. She did not smile. The fan moved overhead. The room felt almost level again, like a table after someone presses down all four legs.

When she left for the office, he opened the drawer and took out the photograph one more time. He looked at the hill behind them and the way the light sat flat on their shoulders. He turned it over. The date remained the same. The words did not alter. He stood with the picture until he heard the watchman's whistle below and the lift's doors opening and closing and the sound of another person's morning. Then he slid the photograph back into the drawer, closed it, and pressed his palm to the wood until the heat from his hand sank in and left no trace.

He changed his phone's unlock pattern to something he could not do without thinking. He deleted three numbers he never answered. He placed his wallet with the folded paper beside the bed and sat on the floor with his back to the wall, the room held together by small decisions that felt like stitches.

When the phone rang again, he let it ring once, then answered. He said yes. He said he would meet. He said a place that was not close to home.

He put on his shoes and picked up his keys, then stopped, turned back, and opened the drawer one more time. He looked at the photograph without touching it, as if the image could hear him. Then he closed the drawer and left, locking the door on the first try.

8

App Notification

She was on the sofa, one leg tucked under her, scrolling absently while the TV ran through some soap she wasn't watching. He was at the table, bills spread like fallen cards, pen in his hand but no numbers written.

Her phone vibrated once. A push notification blinked across the screen.

[Watcher's Notes]

"New activity: [Arjun_30] last seen on Tinder at 21:02 hrs."

She stared at it until it dimmed. She tapped it open again. Same message. Same time stamp.

She didn't speak. She placed the phone face down and lit a cigarette, her movements unhurried. The smoke curled toward the ceiling.

"You're quiet," he said without looking up.

"So are you."

He scribbled a figure onto a bill, scratched it out, wrote nothing else. "Long day."

"Same." She leaned back into the cushions, watching him from behind a veil of smoke.

Later, while he rinsed dishes in the sink, she opened her phone again, careful, tilting it away from his line of sight. The app blinked with the same alert. She closed it, stood, and carried her cup into the kitchen.

"You ever use Tinder?" she asked.

The clink of glass against metal paused, just for a beat. "Why?"

"Just asking."

"Everybody did. Once."

"Once." Her tone was flat, not rising.

He dried his hands on the towel, looked at her. "Why?"

"Curious." She placed the cup in the rack, met his eyes steady, then smiled without showing teeth. "Relax."

That night in bed, she reached for his phone while he showered. The screen lit up at her touch. The pattern had changed. The smudge no longer matched.

When he returned, towelling his hair, she was lying on her side, eyes shut. Her breathing was even, practiced. He set his phone on the table, screen facing him.

She waited until his breaths steadied before opening her eyes again.

The next morning, she slid her phone across the table toward him with his tea. "Play something," she said. "Music."

He picked it up, unlocked it with her code, scrolled. His thumb brushed over her apps. He didn't notice the one at the corner, tucked into a folder, still running. And if he did, he didn't mention it.

"Old Hindi or English?" he asked.

"Surprise me."

He chose something soft, left it playing, slid the phone back. She glanced at the folder. The app was still open, still humming in the background like a wire under the floor.

In the evening, they sat at a café with a view of the street. She ordered tea, he asked for black coffee. While he paid the bill, she leaned closer, her voice low.

"You sure you deleted it?"

"Deleted what?"

She held his gaze. He frowned, reached for his cigarette. "I don't have it anymore."

"Anymore is not never."

He inhaled, exhaled smoke into the street. "You're looking for things."

"Maybe they're looking for me."

47

He stubbed the cigarette, stood, and said nothing else.

Watcher's Notes

[21:02 hrs | Subject M's device activity]

Dating app log-in detected.
Duration: 4 min 11 sec.
Subject F device: alert received.

That night, she didn't reach for him in bed. He rolled closer anyway, arm brushing hers. She stayed still, eyes open in the dark, the fan clicking overhead.

In the silence, suspicion thickened, not spoken, not proved, but present, heavy as another body between them.

9

The Fight

They left the café without finishing their tea. The sky had turned a flat, hard colour, and the air felt charged. He paid in cash. She watched the notes change hands and said nothing.

On the pavement he reached for her hand. She let him take it for three steps, then eased free.

"What now," he said.

"Walk," she said.

A woman with a plastic sheet over her shoulders hurried past. A man balanced an umbrella and a crate of guavas. The traffic at the corner coughed fumes into the heat. The first drop hit her forearm and left a dark mark on her skin.

"Let us take a rickshaw," he said.

"I want to walk."

The drops thickened. A vendor snapped his stall shut with elastic cords. The watchman at their building doorway leaned out and looked up at the sky as if it had changed the plan without asking.

He tried again. "You are angry."

"You are observant," she said.

"Tell me why."

"Tell me why Tinder knows what time you breathe."

He stopped. "We are doing this here."

"Where do you prefer to lie," she said, and kept walking.

They cut across to the lane that ran beside the petrol pump. The first burst of water came down, cold and hard, flattening dust, turning the road into a sheet that reflected headlights. He pulled his shirt collar up. She did not bother. Her hair stuck to her cheeks. She wiped it back with the heel of her hand and kept moving.

"I deleted it," he said.

"And then you logged in at nine oh two."

"I did not."

She took out her phone, turned the screen toward him without stopping. The alert blinked. Last seen. Same time. She slid the phone back into her pocket and shook her head once, a small, tired gesture.

"Maybe it is a bug," he said.

"Your life has many bugs," she said. "I am always the one that gets bitten."

They passed a shuttered salon. A boy in a vest dragged a bucket under the awning and grinned as water filled it in seconds. A car sent a sheet of dirty water up over their shoes. She flinched. He stepped in front of her on instinct and then stepped back when she gave him a look.

"Who is Riya," she said.

He blinked water from his eyelashes. "You know."

"Engaged is a word that sits like furniture. It takes up space." She cut across him with her arm. "And who called you on Carter Road. The polished shoes."

"Drop it."

"Say his name."

"Do not do this here."

"Here is where we are," she said. "Say it."

He said the first name, the smaller one, the one people use for the man who stands between you and a worse man. She exhaled, short and sharp, as if she had guessed and only wanted to make him admit it.

"Good," she said. "Now say you owe him."

"I am working on it."

"You are not."

He stopped under a shop awning and wiped his face with both hands. The water drummed on the plastic above them. She stood just outside the shelter, letting it fall.

"You disappeared a night," he said. "Do I get to ask where."

"You can ask."

"Where."

"Not with that face."

"What face."

"The one that wants to win."

He stepped out from under the awning and back into the street with her. "Who," he said.

She looked him in the eye. "No one who matters to you."

"That is not an answer."

"That is the only one you will understand."

They crossed at the signal. Shoes slipped on the paint. A biker rode too close and swore. They reached the opposite pavement. She shook water from her fingers and moved toward the low wall that ran along the edge of a small park.

"Give me your phone," she said.

"No."

"You had mine."

He hesitated, then handed it over. The screen stayed shut. She waited. He entered the pattern, careful to shield it with his palm. She watched his hand. He saw her watching.

"You changed it again," she said.

"You told me to."

"I told you to change the password to your bank. I did not ask you to build a wall around your lies."

He took the phone back and pocketed it. "Say who last night was."

She sat on the wall, water dripping from her jacket to make a small dark circle on the stone. "A person I knew before you," she said. "Like Riya is a person you knew before me."

"It is not the same."

"It never is when men say it."

He stood in front of her, trying to find a position that made sense. "You want me to tell you the truth. You do not offer yours."

"I offered my life to your screen," she said, and held out her hand for his phone again. "Yours was open when you needed me. Now it is a door with a code you do not say aloud."

"You looked at my drawer," he said.

"You left it open," she said.

"You went through my things."

"You brought me to your life like a guest and then told me not to sit," she said. "Choose."

Two teenagers ran past them barefoot, laughing, hair slicked to their foreheads. Water gurgled into a blocked drain and lifted paper cups and leaves in a slow spiral. A rickshaw pulled up with its plastic flaps pulled down. The driver lifted a hand at them and waited. Neither moved.

He tried to lower his voice. "I am trying," he said. "I am trying to hold the pieces."

"You collect pieces," she said. "Accounts, logins, photographs, debts. You do not hold them. You misplace them and then pretend the room changed."

He felt something inside him give. "You came because you needed somewhere to stay," he said. "Do not make it holy."

She stood. The line landed between them like a dropped plate. For a second no one moved. Then she stepped closer, almost chest to chest, and spoke in a voice soft enough that the driver could not hear.

"Say that again," she said.

He did not. He stepped back, hands open, water dripping from his hair onto his knuckles. She stared at his hands as if the apology might be written there in water.

He tried another tack. "I like you here," he said. "I do not know what that means yet. I am trying to learn it while people knock on my door."

"I like me here too," she said. "I like me more when I do not have to check who else you are."

He swallowed. "It is not like that."

"It is exactly like that."

He reached for her wrist. She pulled away. He reached again and caught her forearm just above the wrist, more to stop her leaving than to hurt. She twisted out of his grip. The skin would hold the shape of his fingers for a minute, then fade.

"Do not touch me to keep me," she said.

He let his hands fall. "Come upstairs," he said. "We are standing in the middle of this."

"We are already in the middle," she said.

A bus took the corner with a slow sweep and pushed water into a wave that surged over the curb. It washed over their shoes and receded. He looked down. She did not.

"Answer me," he said. "Is there someone else."

"You first," she said. "Is there someone still."

He breathed in, breathed out. The air smelled like wet concrete and diesel and fried batter from a stall that refused to close. He nodded, once, small, toward the pocket where his phone sat. She nodded toward the building where the drawer waited.

"Then there it is," she said.

"Then what."

"We stop pretending it is not happening," she said.

"What do you want."

"Honesty," she said. "And if not that, then clarity."

"That is the same thing."

"No," she said. "One is the thing itself. The other is the thing named."

He swallowed rain. "I do not want to lose you."

"You cannot lose what you never had," she said.

He flinched.

The driver in the rickshaw shook his head and pulled away. Two women argued under a bus stop over whose umbrella had kept which shoulder dry. A dog shook itself and trotted to shelter. The street kept making its noise. The fight belonged to the world for a while and then belonged only to them again.

He spoke first. "I did log in," he said. "For a minute. I did not swipe. I did not speak to anyone. I wanted to see if the account still existed."

"You already know the answer," she said.

"I wanted to see if I could end it from there. I could not remember the email."

"You remember everything that keeps you away from consequence," she said.

He nodded, once. "You stayed out that night," he said. "Tell me where."

"In a room that was not yours," she said, and held his eyes. "I slept. I left early. I came home."

"With whom."

"Someone who is not waiting outside our building," she said. "Someone who does not know your name."

He exhaled. It did not help. "Do you want to be with me," he said. "Right now. Not in theory. Not in anger. Yes or no."

She looked at the road, at the moving water, at the mirror of red and white lights sliding across it. She looked back at him. "Yes," she said. "But not like this."

"How then."

"Not as a secret I have to keep for you," she said. "Not as a lie you keep for yourself."

He nodded. He meant it. He did not know how to do it. The water ran down from his hair into his eyes. He blinked it away and tasted the city on his lip. She tucked her wet hair behind her ear and then let it fall again, as if undecided on the gesture.

"Come upstairs," he said again.

"Say you will end it," she said. "Not the app. The other lies."

"I will," he said.

"Say you will tell me when the polished shoes return."

"I will."

"Say you will throw away the photograph."

He paused. She saw it. The pause took less than a breath and more than enough time. She watched his face close a small door and then open a different one.

He tried. "It is only paper."

"Paper cuts," she said. "You bleed before you notice."

He stepped closer. "I will put it away," he said.

"You already did," she said. "That is the problem."

She turned to go. He set his hand on her shoulder lightly, not to stop her, only to ask. She removed it with two fingers, polite as returning a borrowed thing.

"Do not follow me," she said.

"I live in your direction," he said.

"Not tonight."

She walked toward the crossing. The signal changed to red, and the cars sighed to a stop. She stepped off the curb and moved between the idling vehicles. He waited on the pavement, because he could not think of a way to move that did not look like begging.

On the far side she stopped and looked back. She raised her hand, not to wave, only to say she had seen him. Then she turned down the side lane that led to the bus stop and the bakery and the phone recharge shop.

He stayed where he was until she disappeared behind the line of parked cars. Then he walked in the opposite direction, toward the building and the watchman and the lift that always paused one extra second before closing.

The watchman looked up from his stool. "Saab," he said, a question inside the word. He nodded and kept walking.

Upstairs the flat smelled of damp cloth and something fried from a neighbour's kitchen. He closed the door and stood with his back to it. The room felt tilted, as if a leg had been taken from a table.

He toed off his shoes and left them by the door. He peeled his wet shirt away and wrung it over the bathroom sink. Water ran down his arms and into the basin. He washed his face, towelled off, then went to the table and pulled open the drawer.

The photograph lay where he had left it, under the passport, edges a little more softened by time. He took it out and held it at the corners. He waited for the impulse that would tear it. It did not come. He set it on

59

the table and pressed it flat with his palm. When he lifted his hand, a faint wet print marked one corner and then evaporated.

His phone buzzed. He picked it up. A message from an unknown number. He did not open it. He set the phone face down. He turned off the overhead light and let the smaller lamp throw a circle across the table. He stood in the edge of that circle and listened to the lift moving up and down the building, to the pipes talking behind the walls, to the quiet that arrived and stayed.

He locked the door, then unlocked it, then locked it again. He returned to the table and sat, hands on his knees, shoulders curved like a man waiting for a wave.

The room settled around him. The clock on the wall kept the slow beat it always kept. He counted four turns of the fan, then stopped counting. He picked up the photograph again and turned it over. The date had not changed. The words had not changed. He held it up and looked through the white margin to the lamplight beyond, as if light could thin memory.

He put the photograph back in the drawer and closed it until the wood sat flush. He stood and crossed to the window and pulled the curtain an inch to one side. The street below shone and moved. A rickshaw cut a V of spray. The watchman leaned under the building lip and smoked. On the third-floor opposite, a rectangle of light went dark and then bright again, someone testing a switch.

His phone vibrated once more. He opened it. A transaction failed alert. Another message from the same number. He closed the notifications without reading. He went to the bathroom and let water run over his hands until the sound calmed him. He turned the tap off. The silence was louder after.

He lay on the bed on his back and stared at the ceiling until the ticking of the fan faded into the noise outside. When sleep finally came it did not stay.

[22:16 hrs | Chapel Road, corner near petrol pump]

Verbal altercation observed.
Subjects separated at 22:12 hrs.
Subject F exited via east lane. Subject M
returned to residence.
Public witnesses present.

He woke before morning and found the room as he had left it. The drawer shut. The phone face down. The shirt still damp over the chair. He sat up and pressed his fingers to the place on the table where the photograph had rested. There was nothing to feel. He stood, dressed, and left the flat without checking if he had taken his keys. At the gate the watchman nodded at him as if they had spoken already.

On the lane he looked for her without intending to. He did not see her. He walked to the bakery and bought bread he did not want. He walked past the bus stop and the recharge shop and back again. He stood at the crossing where they had spoken and watched the signal change to red and then to green and then to red again.

He took out his phone and opened the app store. He typed the name he had deleted. He stared at the screen. He put the phone away. He crossed the street with the others. He went home and made tea and did not drink it.

The doorbell rang once. He held his breath and went to the door. Through the peephole a blurred figure. He opened it.

The polished shoes were dry.

10

The Disappearance

He woke to silence. Not the kind that belongs to morning, but the kind that follows something leaving.

The bed beside him was empty. The sheet still carried her warmth, but faint, fading. Her jacket was gone from the chair. The slippers by the bed were missing.

He sat up, rubbed his eyes, listened for water running in the bathroom. Nothing.

He checked the kitchen. The mugs were clean, lined side by side on the rack. The ashtray had been emptied. A note would have been ordinary. There was no note.

He called once. No answer.

He called again. The ring carried, then cut into voicemail. He stared at the screen as if the numbers could explain her silence.

By noon he had paced the flat enough times that the carpet had begun to show faint paths. He left the TV on for noise, muted. He opened the fridge and closed it again without touching anything.

At two p.m. he called again. Still no answer.

By evening, the flat had grown heavy with her absence. He stood by the window, smoking, watching the opposite building. Curtains swayed. A child bounced a ball against the railing. On the third floor, a figure stood too long at the window before stepping back into shadow.

He let the curtain fall.

At work the next day, his phone stayed face-up on the desk. Colleagues spoke numbers and deadlines around him, but he caught nothing. He checked his screen every two minutes, waiting for a reply that didn't arrive.

At lunch, he walked out into the street, called again. No answer. His reflection in a shop window looked tired, jaw tight, shirt collar bent. He saw the version of himself he had been before her: alone, strained, a man already braced for loss.

That night he went to her place. He had never been inside without her. The watchman at the gate gave him a look, half-curious, half-knowing. Upstairs, the door was locked. He knocked once, then again. Nothing.

The corridor was quiet, only the hum of a ceiling fan from the next flat. He leaned against the wall and waited. Ten minutes passed. Fifteen. No one came.

He slid down, sitting with his back to the door, listening for sounds inside. There were none.

The third day, he began to imagine her absence as deliberate. A punishment, maybe. A test.

He remembered the words she had said in the rain. *You cannot lose what you never had.*

He turned the drawer open again. The photograph waited, unchanged. He closed it with a sharper push this time, the sound too loud in the small flat.

That evening, his phone buzzed. Not her. The polished shoes.

"We should talk," the voice said.

"Not now."

"Now," the man said. "Before it gets worse."

He ended the call, leaned his forehead against the cool wall. Worse had already arrived.

He lay awake, staring at the ceiling. Every sound in the building felt like her return. The lift's whine, a door shutting, a footstep in the corridor. Each one pulled him up, heart jumping, before dropping back into silence.

At four a.m. he lit another cigarette and sat by the window. The city locked too still. A police jeep rolled past at the corner, lights off, engine low. He watched it until it turned out of sight.

[Watcher's Notes]

[04:11 hrs | Subject M's residence]

Subject F absence recorded, 72 hrs duration.
Subject M repeated call attempts (12).
Subject M observed visiting Subject F residence. Access denied.
External contact: Male, identified as debt associate.
Assessment: Subject F unaccounted.
Surveillance escalated.

By the fourth day he had stopped calling. He sat in the café where they had once argued over sugar, stared at the table, ordered coffee he didn't drink.

The waiter asked if she was coming. He said no.

When he returned to his flat that night, the lock looked the same, but the air inside felt altered, like someone had entered and left without touching anything.

He searched the rooms without admitting he was searching. Checked the bathroom, the cupboards, under the bed. Nothing was missing. Nothing was added. Only the smell: faint jasmine, fading.

He called again anyway, one last time. The ring carried, steady. No answer.

He placed the phone on the table, screen glowing in the dim light, and sat with his head in his hands until the glow timed out and left him in darkness.

11

The Watcher

The rain had stopped, but the air stayed damp. The city smelled of wet iron and rotting leaves. He hadn't slept much. Three nights of calling into nothing had left his voice raw, his eyes ringed with purple.

That morning, he shaved, slowly, staring at the mirror as though it might tell him if she was gone for good. His phone lay silent on the counter. He wanted it to buzz, to prove she existed somewhere beyond his own memory.

At the door, he hesitated before locking. For the first time, he pressed the bolt twice, then tugged to check. When he came back in later that evening, the bolt resisted, not stiff, but as if it had been touched.

She returned the next night. No key. She knocked, once, then again, light, as if testing whether he would answer.

He opened, relief and anger tangled in his throat. "Where were you."

She brushed past him, dropped her bag on the chair, pulled her jacket off. "Work."

"You expect me to believe that."

"You expect me to answer more than that."

The silence stretched. She lit a cigarette, sat on the ledge, blew smoke into the night. He leaned against the table, watching the scar on her lip glow each time the ember flared.

"You changed the lock," she said.

"I didn't."

"You checked it twice."

He didn't answer.

Later, in bed, she turned her face away from him. He reached for her shoulder. She shifted slightly, not away, not closer.

"You left without telling me," he whispered.

"I came back," she said.

"You think that's enough."

"It has to be," she said.

The next day, they walked together to the café. She ordered her usual. He didn't speak much, kept glancing at the street outside. At one point she leaned closer, her lips almost brushing the rim of his glass.

"You keep looking over your shoulder," she said.

"Someone was there last night," he said. "In the corridor."

"There's always someone in the corridor."

"Not standing that still."

She shrugged. "Maybe they were listening to us fight."

"Maybe they weren't."

That evening, the power cut out in the flat. Darkness pressed against the walls. He searched for the matches. She held her phone up, screen glowing pale blue, casting shadows that seemed to move too quickly.

"Don't stand by the window," he said.

"Why not."

"They can see in."

"Who."

He didn't answer.

[Watcher's Notes | Day 11]

Subject F returned to Subject M's residence, 20:14 hrs.
Duration of absence: 93 hrs, 22 mins.
Subject M displayed agitation (pacing, repeated lock-checking).
Interaction: raised voices, prolonged silence, resumed cohabitation.
Observation range: interior visual confirmed. Curtains

inadequate.
Recommendation: escalate to close-range monitoring.

The water came back to the pipes with a sudden groan. The fan whirred as the electricity returned. They sat on opposite sides of the room, both pretending to scroll through their phones. Neither reading. Neither moving.

He spoke first. "Do you ever feel it."

She looked up. "Feel what."

"Like we're not the only ones in this room."

She tapped ash into the tray. "You're tired."

"Answer me."

She exhaled smoke slowly, eyes not leaving his. "Yes."

That night, he dreamed of footsteps in the hall. When he woke, the flat was silent, but his skin felt watched. He reached for her. She wasn't there. He sat up, heart pounding, listening. A faint creak. A door hinge. Not theirs. Somewhere close.

He opened the curtain an inch. Across the street, the window opposite was dark. Then light, briefly. Then dark again.

He let the curtain fall.

In the morning, she was in the kitchen, boiling water. She looked rested. He felt raw.

"Do you want tea," she asked.

"Yes."

"You should shave," she said.

He touched his jaw. "I shaved yesterday."

She turned off the stove, poured the water into two cups. "Then shave again."

They drank in silence. The tea was too hot, too bitter. He didn't mind. He needed the burn. She blew on hers, then looked at him over the rim.

"Do you want me to stay here tonight," she asked.

"Yes."

"You think it's safer with me here."

"Yes."

Her eyes flicked to the window. "Then close the curtains."

12

Blood on the Balcony

The morning began ordinary. Street vendors shouting, pressure cooker whistles leaking into corridors, the watchman thumping rolled newspapers against doors.

He made tea. She leaned against the sink, hair pulled back, bare feet cold against the tiles.

"You slept," she said.

"I didn't," he said.

"Your eyes did."

She blew on her cup, lips against the rim. The scar looked sharper in daylight.

They drank without talking. The city pressed in with its noise. The flat felt almost steady.

Until the scream.

It cut up from below, jagged, high, pulling people out of their routines. He dropped his cup; it rolled, spilling across the floor. She froze, head tilted, listening. The scream came again, closer now, joined by voices.

He went to the balcony. She followed.

The building opposite. Third floor. Curtains open. A crowd of faces at the railing, bodies leaning out.

And on the cement below, sprawled, broken. Blood running in a dark fan across the balcony slab, dripping steady through the gaps in the iron grille.

A woman.

Her arm bent wrong. Her hair matted, half her face hidden.

Neighbours shouted. Someone called for the watchman, someone else for the police. Phones lifted, cameras clicked.

He stepped back from the rail, breath shallow. She leaned forward, eyes narrowed, studying the scene as though it belonged to them.

"Who is it," he asked.

"Not me," she said, almost a whisper.

The corridor filled fast. Doors open, slippers shuffling, voices echoing up the stairwell. A boy pushed past him to get a better look. Someone knocked on their door, asking if they had seen. He didn't answer.

She lit a cigarette with steady hands. "Come inside," she said.

They shut the curtains. The flat turned dim. His tea still spread in a puddle across the floor. He wiped it with a rag, hand trembling.

"She fell," he said.

"She was pushed," she said.

"You don't know that."

"You don't know she fell."

He sat, rag still in his hand. She stood at the window, pulling the curtain aside a fraction. "They'll come ask questions," she said.

He nodded. "And you'll tell them…"

"That I don't know her."

"You've seen her?"

Her eyes flicked once. "Maybe."

When the knock came, it was sharp, official. Two men, plainclothes, one with a notebook.

"Did you hear anything," the first asked.

"A scream," he said.

"Did you know the woman."

"No."

The man looked at her. "Madam."

She shook her head. "No."

The second officer wrote something in the book. "We'll be back."

When they left, she exhaled smoke into the curtain's fabric.

"They'll be back," she repeated.

That night the building was restless. People gathered in the courtyard, murmuring. The watchman kept retelling what he saw. Some said suicide. Some whispered murder.

She sat cross-legged on the bed, scrolling her phone. He stood at the sink, washing cups again and again.

"She looked familiar," he said finally.

She didn't look up. "Everyone does when they're dead."

He turned, water dripping from his hands. "Did you know her."

She met his eyes, slow. "Would it matter if I did."

At two a.m. he woke to movement. She wasn't in bed. He found her on the balcony, cigarette glowing, eyes locked on the opposite building. Police tape stretched across the third-floor door. A dark stain remained on the slab below.

She didn't look back when he stepped out.

"Come inside," he said.

She exhaled. "Do you ever wonder if we're next."

[Watcher's Notes| Day 14]

Incident: Female body recovered, Opposite
Building, 03 level balcony.
Cause: impact trauma. Official narrative:
under investigation.
Subjects: M and F observed at rail during
discovery, 08:14 hrs.
Subject F noted continued visual contact
post-incident.
Interaction: limited verbal exchange,
physical agitation.
Assessment: Probability of association
elevated. Surveillance perimeter extended.

The following evening, her mood sharpened. She dressed for work, heels clicking, lipstick bright. At the door she paused.

"They'll be watching," she said.

"Who," he asked.

"Everyone."

She left without kissing him.

He stayed in, lights low, staring at the stain across the way. The balcony was scrubbed now, but the shadow remained. He lit cigarette after cigarette, filling the flat with smoke until the fan could not push it out.

At midnight she still hadn't returned. He dialled her number. Straight to voicemail.

The sound of the fan above him seemed louder. The walls closer.

He wondered whose blood had marked the balcony, hers, or the next woman's, or eventually, his.

13

Police Interrogation

The room was not big. One table, two metal chairs, one fan that clicked every fourth turn. A coil of mosquito mat smouldered in the corner. The paint near the door had bubbled, as if heat had once tried to leave through it.

He sat with his wrists on the table. A paper cup of tea sweated a ring. Across from him, an officer with a square face and a shaved head read from a thin file and did not look up.

"Name," the officer said, though the form already had it.

He answered. The pen scratched.

"Address."

He answered again. The pen paused over the last digit, then moved on.

"You know why you are here."

"I live opposite," he said. "Everyone saw something."

The officer looked up. His eyes were the flat brown of office furniture. "Everyone did not stand at the balcony for ten minutes."

"I heard a scream."

"And then."

"I looked."

"And then."

"Nothing," he said. "Police came. We shut the curtain."

"Your curtain is thin," the officer said. "We know what people do behind thin curtains."

He said nothing.

The officer tapped the file. "She is your girlfriend."

He said nothing again.

"Say yes," the officer said. "Make it easy."

"Yes," he said.

"How long."

He counted days in his head and then stopped. "Three weeks."

The officer made a small sound that could have been a laugh. "Fast," he said.

The fan ticked. The door opened. Another officer placed a steel plate with Glucose biscuits on the table and left. The square-faced officer pushed the plate toward him. "Eat."

He shook his head.

"Eat," the officer said again, not insisting, only saying. He took a biscuit and broke it without meaning to. The crumbs looked like pale sand on the metal.

"You know the dead woman," the officer asked.

"No."

"You know her name."

"No."

"You fight with her."

"No."

The officer turned a page. "Your watchman says you fight with many."

"That is unkind," he said.

"It is accurate," the officer said. "Last night."

"We argued," he said.

"With the dead woman."

"With my girlfriend," he said. "On the road."

"In the rain."

"Yes."

"What time did you reach home."

He thought of the red signal, the bus, the rickshaw, the watchman's nod. "After ten."

The officer wrote it down. "Ten what."

"Sixteen," he said, guessing.

The officer looked at him for a breath, then wrote nothing. "Your phone location says ten twenty-one."

He nodded, as if corrected kindly. "Ten twenty-one."

The officer watched him the way a person watches a drawer to see if it opens on its own. "Your girlfriend," he said, "left you on the road."

"She went the other way."

"And then."

"I went home."

"And then," the officer said again.

"I sat."

The officer closed the file. "You have debts."

He swallowed tea that had cooled. "Yes."

"People come asking."

"Sometimes."

"Names."

He gave the smaller one. The officer waited. He did not give the larger one.

"Phone," the officer said. He placed it on the table. "Unlock."

81

He drew the pattern, slower than usual. The officer slid the phone to himself, scrolled without changing his face. "You use dating apps," he said.

"I deleted them."

"You logged in at nine oh two," the officer said, neutral as a clock. "Why."

"To delete," he said.

The officer's mouth tilted. Not a smile. "We will take the phone," he said. "Sit."

The door opened again. A younger constable leaned in. "Sir."

The officer stood. "Wait," he told him, and left.

He sat alone with the fan and the crumbs and the ring of tea.

Through the wall a voice rose, clipped, a woman's voice answering low, then higher. He could not hear the words. He did not need to. He knew the pattern of her answers.

He wiped the ring of tea with his thumb and then wiped his thumb on his jeans. The fan ticked.

In the next room the light was colder. A lady officer with a braid under her cap sat with a ledger open, a line of dates on the left margin in careful blue.

"Name," she said.

She answered.

"Where were you last night."

"Home."

"Not your home," the officer said. "His."

"Yes."

"What time did you leave him."

"Ten," she said.

"Not the fight," the officer said. "After."

"I did not leave after," she said. "I left then."

"You went where."

"Home."

"Your own."

"Yes."

"Which route."

She named the road, then the side lane, then the bus stop with the bakery and the recharge shop.

"What time did you reach."

"Ten thirty."

"Phone shows ten forty-eight at your building gate," the officer said. "Battery drained. Or story."

She made her face into a calm place. "Battery," she said.

"Why did you switch off later."

"I slept."

"You do not switch off to sleep," the officer said. "You switch off to hide."

She folded her hands in her lap. Her nails were short, clean. "I slept," she said again.

"Do you know the dead woman."

"No."

The officer turned the ledger so the page faced her. A printout of a photograph was taped crooked across the line. Third floor balcony. Police tape. The body already covered, a shoe fallen near the rail. In the background, a woman's face behind a grille, blurred but not enough. A scar glinting faintly on a lip.

The officer tapped the image. "This is you."

"I live opposite," she said.

"Everyone lives opposite," the officer said. "Not everyone leans out."

"She screamed," she said.

"You smoke a lot," the officer said, as if it were about the photograph. "Your fingers are yellow at the tips."

She looked at her fingers. "Yes."

"Did you know the woman," the officer said again.

She looked at the ledger instead of the photograph. "No."

The officer flipped a plastic folder open. A smaller image, pulled from the same balcony, a day earlier, a group of people at the railing during a different commotion, a small boy calling for his ball. In the group the dead woman stood alive, profile sharp, hair tied, a ring catching light.

"Do you know her now."

"No."

"What do you do for work."

"Marketing."

"His work."

"Finance," she said.

"Debt," the officer said. She did not ask. She said it as if saying weather.

She said nothing.

"You were gone three nights," the officer said. "He called twelve times."

"I was working."

"Your office says you did not swipe in," the officer said, patient as the ledger line. "You did not use your laptop either. You changed a password. You changed another."

She tucked hair behind her ear. "I was not at my desk," she said.

"Where."

"Friends."

"Which friend."

"Private," she said.

The officer smiled a little. "Not here."

She looked at the photograph again. The shoe. The edge of the rail. The place where the blood had been scrubbed.

"Do you want a lawyer," the officer asked.

"Do I need one," she said.

The officer closed the ledger halfway. "We always ask," she said.

"I will answer," she said.

"Unlock your phone," the officer said.

She placed it on the table and tapped the numbers. The officer scrolled. She watched the way the officer held the device by its edges, careful not to leave prints. The officer opened an app folder labelled Utilities. Inside, a dating app ID pinged once in the history and then stopped. The officer looked up.

"He logged in at nine oh two," the officer said. "Who told you."

"It is my phone," she said.

"You installed the alert."

She said nothing.

"You do not like to be surprised," the officer said.

"Not anymore," she said.

The officer's pen wrote something down she could not see. The lady officer looked up again, softened her voice without making it kind. "Did you know her," she said a third time.

"No," she said. "I knew the scream." She kept her eyes on the officer's face, steady. "Is that enough for today."

The officer tapped the screen off and slid the phone back two inches. Not enough to be hers. "We will keep it," she said.

"For how long."

"Until we like you more," the officer said, still pleasant.

She smiled without showing teeth. "That may take time."

The officer smiled back with the same mouth.

Back in his room the square-faced officer returned and sat. He placed two printouts on the table, side by side.

One was a screenshot of building CCTV, grainy, time stamp in the corner. The other was a call log.

"You returned at ten twenty-one," the officer said. "You did not go out again."

"I did not."

"You receive a message at ten fifty," the officer said. "From an unknown number."

He nodded.

"You receive another at eleven twenty-three," the officer said. "You delete it."

"I did not," he said.

The officer pushed the printout closer with one finger. "You did," he said. "You delete many things."

He looked at the paper and saw nothing he could read. He pressed his thumbs together to keep them from shaking.

"You have a photograph," the officer said. "In your drawer."

He stayed very still.

"You keep it because you do not like endings," the officer said. "You think paper makes a person stay."

"It is old," he said.

"Everything is old by the time it breaks," the officer said. "Where were you at nine twelve."

"Café," he said.

"With whom."

"Her."

"She left you on the road," the officer said. "She went east. You went north. The dead woman fell south."

He blinked.

The officer sat back as if a show had ended. "Tell me something I want to write down," he said.

He wanted to say he knew nothing. He wanted to say it cleanly, in a voice with no cracks. "We fought," he said instead. "She left. I went home. I smoked. I slept. I woke up early. That is all."

The officer waited one more second, then stood. "Give me your passcode for banking," he said.

He flinched. "Why."

"Debt leaves marks," the officer said. "We look for marks."

"I do not know if I can."

"You can," the officer said. "Write."

He did not write.

The officer did not move. The fan ticked. The mosquito mat burned in its coil and let out a sweet, chemical ghost.

He wrote.

The officer folded the paper and slipped it inside the file. "Thank you," he said, in a tone that made the word feel new.

They put them in the same corridor after, on two benches with a white line of paint between. He looked at the floor. She looked at the notice board with faded posters about helpline numbers and how to file an FIR.

He said nothing. She said nothing. A constable walked by with a bundle of files tied with a red string. The bundle looked like a story that had learned to keep its mouth shut.

She turned her head slightly. "They kept your phone," she said.

"They kept yours," he said.

She nodded once, as if they had agreed on something important.

A woman with henna on her hands cried on the next bench. A boy brought her water. The water spilled and left the shape of a country on the tile before it dried.

A young officer with a neat moustache appeared and said her name. She stood.

"One more question," he told her. "Only one."

She followed him back into the cold light. The lady officer waited with the ledger open again.

"You were absent three nights," the lady officer said. "He called twelve times."

"I know," she said.

"Where were you."

"Not with the dead woman," she said.

"That is not the question," the lady officer said.

"It is the answer I have." she said.

The lady officer closed the ledger fully now. "We will call you again," she said.

"For what."

"To see if your answer changes."

"It will not," she said.

"We know," the lady officer said.

They let him out last. The square-faced officer handed him a receipt for his phone and a separate paper with lines for signatures.

"You will not go out of the city," the officer said.

"I work here," he said.

"You will answer when we call," the officer said.

"I always do," he said.

The officer looked at him for a beat. "You do not," he said. "Do not teach me my job."

He nodded.

At the door the officer stopped him with a word said low. "Look at me," he said. He looked.

"Do not lie in small ways," the officer said. "It makes the big lies look cheap."

He went down the station stairs into a light that made the dust on the road look like glitter from far away. She was on the footpath, arms folded, hair tied high to keep off the heat. They stood two meters apart. People passed between them as if they were not there.

"They kept the phones," she said.

"They will call," he said.

"We are not to leave the city," she said.

"We do not have anywhere to go," he said.

She almost smiled. "Speak for yourself," she said.

They began to walk without saying where. A vendor shouted about lemons. A man argued about a helmet. A girl on a scooter laughed with her mouth open and her head thrown back.

He touched his pocket and met only cloth. He felt smaller without the weight of the metal rectangle. She seemed lighter without hers.

At the gate a constable watched them through mirrored sunglasses. The reflection made them look as if they were walking backward.

[11:30 hrs | Interview Rooms 1–2]

Subjects interviewed separately.
Contradictions logged: time of return, device status, absence duration.
Both surrendered devices for forensic review.
Release on instruction. Movement restrictions advised.

They sat at a tea stall near the corner, paper cups between their fingers. He stirred sugar into his though he hated it. She watched the spoon turn.

"What did you tell them," he said.

"The truth that fits," she said.

"And the rest."

She drank, then set the cup down. "I did not give them a name," she said.

He nodded. "Me neither."

Her eyes dropped to his empty hand, the way his thumb worked the air as if a phone still lived there. "You will not log in at nine oh two anymore," she said, gentle as a scratch.

"I will not," he said.

"You will not keep photographs in drawers," she said.

"I will not."

"You will tell me when polished shoes knock," she said.

"I will."

She picked up her cup and tilted the last of the tea. The dregs slid and left a brown crescent. She looked at it as if it said something.

"They will come to the building again," she said.

"I know."

"They will ask the neighbours."

"I know."

"They will ask the watchman."

He looked at the station gate. "He will tell them we fight."

"We do," she said.

He looked at her. "We do."

They sat with the empty cups until the boy asked if they wanted more. She said no. He said no. They got up at the same time and walked toward the lane, matching each other's pace without meaning to. At the corner she stopped.

"Your place or mine," she said, with no humour, no invitation, only the map.

"Yours," he said. "Let us see if the lock still turns."

They crossed the road and did not talk. The city rushed around them as if in a hurry to forget.

When they reached her building the watchman looked at them with the careful blankness of a man who had decided not to have an opinion. She took the stairs. He followed. On the landing she paused and turned her head toward the window that gave a view of the opposite balcony. The stain had faded to a shadow.

"Do you think she jumped," he asked, low.

She pressed her palm to the wall for balance. "I think someone wanted it to look like that," she said.

He looked at her hand on the wall, at the way her fingers spread, as if reading a temperature. "Who," he asked.

She took her hand away, then put it in her pocket. "I do not know yet," she said. "Maybe we do not have to know. Maybe it is enough that someone knows we do not."

They climbed the last flight in silence. At her door she turned the key and pushed. The bolt stuck for a second, then gave. The flat smelled of closed air and the last time she had been here. Nothing looked moved. Still, they both stood and listened, as if the space itself might answer whether they were alone.

He closed the door and slid the latch. She went to the window and pulled the curtain until it met the other edge. The room dimmed.

"Tea," she said.

"Yes," he said.

She filled the kettle. He found cups. They moved without asking where what was.

When the water boiled, she poured. He held his cup and did not drink. She stood beside him and did not drink either. They looked at the steam rise and vanish.

"Do you think they believe us," he asked.

"They believe themselves," she said.

In the quiet that followed, the building made its small noises. A child ran along a corridor and stumbled and laughed. Someone dropped a spoon. A door closed. The fan clicked on the fourth turn.

They sipped tea that had gone warm. He set his cup down. She set hers down too. They stood closer without noticing and watched the curtain breathe with the draft under the door.

The city outside went on cataloguing everything. Inside, they tried not to make any new marks.

14

The Apartment as Witness

The flat had changed.

Not in furniture, not in paint. In weight. The walls seemed to carry sound longer, as if listening. The table, once just a table, now held questions, lies, photographs that should have burned. Even the fan's click had grown louder, a reminder on every fourth turn.

They moved through it like tenants in someone else's house, careful, rehearsed. She brewed tea slower. He folded clothes that had never been folded before. Their silences touched more than their words did.

That night she sat by the window, curtain half-drawn, a cigarette between her fingers. He lay on the sofa with the TV on mute, watching light flash across her face.

"You think they'll come again," he asked.

"They don't have to," she said. "They're already here."

He looked at the opposite building. A balcony door was open, curtain moving in the draft. Just air, he told himself. Just air.

She blew smoke, let it curl against the glass. "Your lock is stiff," she said.

"I oiled it."

"Not enough."

He sat up. "You want to go back to your place?"

She exhaled. "This place remembers too much," she said.

The next morning, he woke before her. The bed felt warmer, heavier with her presence, but the silence between them had grown like a crack in plaster. He dressed quietly, found his wallet, paused by the drawer.

He did not open it. He pressed his hand flat on the wood, felt its pulse, then left.

When he returned at noon she was gone. A mug stood on the sink, half-drained, the rim smudged with her lipstick. The curtain was still drawn, but the ashtray on the ledge was full. He emptied it, washed the mug, wiped the counter, as though erasing evidence.

The flat smelled fainter every day.

In the evening, she came back with groceries. He reached for the bag. She let him take it, then walked straight to the window, pulled the curtain wider, looked out.

"What are you checking for," he asked.

"Myself," she said.

He followed her gaze. A man across the street stood smoking, elbows on the rail, face half-hidden in shadow. Could have been anyone. Could have been no one.

"You see him too," she said.

"Yes."

They stood a long time until the man flicked his cigarette and walked away.

The days blurred. They worked side by side on laptops, drank tea, shared cigarettes. Ordinary things, but the ordinary carried an edge now.

At night, he would lie awake, listening for steps outside. She would smoke until the room filled, then open the window just enough for the smell to leave, not enough for eyes to enter.

Once, at three a.m., the lift doors opened and closed without footsteps. They both sat up in bed. Neither spoke. They listened until the fan's click swallowed the silence again.

[Watcher's Notes| Day 18]

Interior surveillance sustained.
Subject F activity: frequent balcony checks, window curtain adjustments.
Subject M activity: repeated drawer interaction without object removal.
Flat environment: high tobacco residue, abnormal nocturnal alertness.
Assessment: psychological stress indicators present. Apartment remains primary witness site.

On the fifth day after interrogation, the neighbours stopped greeting them. The old woman from 2B, who usually asked about milk deliveries, turned her face away in the stairwell. The watchman gave shorter nods. Whispers moved faster than the lift.

She noticed it first. "They've started counting," she said.

"Counting what."

"Our steps. Our lights. Our nights in and out."

"They'll forget," he said.

"They never forget," she said.

The flat absorbed their quarrels differently now. Voices echoed longer, bounced sharper off the walls. After an argument, the silence stayed thick, as if the room replayed the words back to them.

One night, she slammed the bathroom door. He followed, stood outside.

"You think this is about the police," she said from behind it.

"What else is it."

"It's about us being a story they can tell. A bad one."

He pressed his forehead to the door. "Then what are we."

She opened it suddenly. He almost fell forward. Her eyes were dry, cold. "We're the footnote before the body," she said.

On the seventh day, he found her standing by the table, drawer open. The photograph lay outside, face up.

"You left it again," she said.

"I didn't touch it."

"It's out," she said, voice flat.

"Maybe you…"

"Don't."

She picked it up, turned it over. "Always, Riya," she read. "You never corrected that."

He reached for it. She pulled her hand back.

"This flat has better memory than you," she said.

He stared at her hand, at the photograph trembling faintly in her grip.

"Put it away," he said.

She slid it back, shut the drawer slow, as though teaching him how to close a thing properly.

That night, the ceiling fan stopped mid-turn. Silence thickened until the flat seemed to breathe with them. Then the fan ticked, started again.

He whispered, "You hear it."

She said nothing.

In the dark, the flat felt awake, listening.

15

Secrets Surface

The call came when she was in the shower. He let it ring twice before answering.

"Payment," the voice said. No name, no greeting.

"I said I'm arranging."

"You said that last week."

"I'll have it."

"Three days," the voice said, then cut.

He stared at the black screen, then at the bathroom door. The sound of water masked his breathing. He placed the phone face down.

When she came out, towelling her hair, he was at the window smoking. She smelled the lie in the air even before he spoke.

"Wrong number," he said.

"Always," she replied.

Later that evening she found the envelope. It wasn't hidden, only slipped between the pages of an old magazine under the sofa. A demand letter. Final notice. The figure circled in red.

When he came back from the balcony she was holding it.

"You want to tell me," she said.

His face tightened. "Not now."

"When then."

"When I fix it."

She folded the paper once, then again, until it was small enough to disappear in her fist. "You don't fix things. You hide them."

He reached for it. She kept her hand closed.

"Give it," he said.

"No."

"Give it."

She tucked her fist into her pocket. "You're not the only one with ghosts," she said.

The next morning, he woke to her side of the bed empty again. Panic shot through him, until he saw her slipper still by the door. She hadn't gone far.

He found her on the staircase, smoking in her nightdress, bare feet against the cold stone.

"What are you doing here," he asked.

104

"Listening," she said.

"For what."

"The neighbours. The whispers. Us."

He sat two steps below her. "You want me to explain."

"No," she said. "I want you to stop pretending I don't already know.

That evening, she left her phone unlocked on the table while she showered. A message flashed. A name he didn't recognize. *Are you safe?*

He picked it up, thumb hovering, but didn't scroll further. He set it back exactly where it was.

When she came out, she saw the way he looked at her phone.

"Say it," she said.

"Who was that."

"Someone who doesn't owe polished shoes," she said.

"That's not an answer."

"It's the only one you'll get tonight."

They fought without raising their voices. Their words were sharper that way.

"You think I don't see," he said.

"You think I don't hear," she said.

"Who is he."

"Who is she."

"That photograph means nothing."

"Neither does a name on a screen."

The fight ended when the lights flickered. They stood in sudden darkness, breath loud in the silence. The bulb came back on, humming.

She said quietly, "This flat is listening."

[Watcher's Notes| Day 21]

Subject M contacted by debt associate.
Payment deadline set: 72 hrs.
Subject F external contact confirmed.
Message: "Are you safe."
Interaction between subjects:
confrontation, withheld disclosures.
Apartment tension: elevated. Surveillance
perimeter holding.

The next night, he followed her. Not far, not clever, just half a block behind as she walked fast through Bandra's crowded lane. She entered a narrow café lit by hanging bulbs.

Through the glass he saw her sit with a man in a plain shirt. Middle-aged, hair receding, voice low. She leaned forward, listening, then touched his hand once. Not tender, not romantic, but steady.

He stood outside until she looked up and saw him. Her eyes didn't flinch. She turned back to the man, finished her cigarette, then rose.

When she came out, she didn't speak. She walked past him as if the city had given her another direction.

He followed anyway.

At home she shut the door, dropped her bag, lit another cigarette.

"You followed me," she said.

"You didn't hide."

"Maybe I wanted you to see."

"Who is he."

"A name you wouldn't believe if I said it."

"Try me."

She exhaled smoke, eyes narrowing. "My brother."

He blinked. "You don't have a brother."

"That's what I tell people," she said.

They didn't speak for hours after. He lay on the bed, staring at the ceiling fan's slow turn. She sat at the window, ashtray filling.

Just before dawn, she said, "You think I'm lying."

"Yes."

She turned, the scar on her lip catching the thin light. "Good. Because maybe I am."

The flat grew heavier with what they weren't saying. The walls had heard enough to know both were keeping pieces back. It wasn't love holding them now. It was the gravity of shared lies.

16

The Betrayal

The deadline loomed. Three days, polished shoes had said. The number sat like rust in his head.

He counted cash on the table again and again, the notes never changing, never enough. She watched from the window, cigarette balanced between two fingers.

"You keep adding the same numbers," she said.

"They have to grow sometime."

"They don't," she said.

He slammed the drawer shut. The photograph inside rattled. She flinched at the sound.

That night she slipped out. He knew because the bolt made a soft scrape when it turned. He didn't stop her.

When she returned, her jacket was damp, hair smelling faintly of another man's smoke. She dropped her bag on the chair and sat without speaking.

"Where," he asked.

"Not here," she said.

"That's not an answer."

"It's the only one you'll get."

The next morning, he found his phone moved an inch on the table. He hadn't touched it.

When he opened the drawer, the photograph was gone. He searched the room in silence, heart racing, until he found it tucked back inside, slightly bent.

She came out of the bathroom, towel around her hair, and saw him holding it.

"You left it," he said.

"You keep saying that," she said.

"You want me to think you never touched it."

She shrugged, eyes steady. "Maybe I want you to think I know her."

On the second day, polished shoes waited again outside the building. This time she went down to meet him. He saw them from the balcony, her back straight, her arms folded, the man's hands gesturing sharp. She didn't step away when he leaned close.

When she came back upstairs, she smelled of rain and cigarettes.

"What did he want," he asked.

"You."

"And you went."

"Someone has to."

That night she didn't share his bed. She lay on the sofa, light still on, scrolling her phone. He lay awake in the bedroom, staring at the fan.

At 2 a.m. the lift opened and closed again. He sat up, heart hammering, waited for footsteps. None came.

He went to the door, peered through the peephole. The corridor was empty. When he turned back, she was standing behind him, cigarette glowing.

"You're jumpy," she said.

"You make me," he said.

On the third day, she left early. He followed again, careful this time, a block behind. She met the same man in the café. They didn't touch, but they leaned too close. Papers exchanged hands, folded, slipped into her bag.

He stepped away before she could spot him, but his pulse carried the image back home: her bag, heavy with someone else's secrets.

That evening, she came in calm, almost gentle. She set the bag down, poured two cups of tea, handed him one.

"You've been quiet," she said.

"You too."

They sat opposite, sipping in silence. The curtain stirred with the draft, the room thick with smoke.

He set his cup down. "Who is he."

She looked at him for a long moment, then said, "The one who can save you."

He almost laughed. "From what."

"From yourself."

"Then why do I feel like you're saving him from me."

She leaned back, scar catching the light. "Because maybe I am."

That night, when he searched her bag, he found the envelope. Not money, documents. Photocopies of his debt notices, his bank records, even his passport.

He stared at the stack, heart racing. She had taken everything that could name him.

She came out of the bathroom, hair damp, and saw the papers in his hands.

"You went through my bag," she said.

"You went through my life," he said.

Her lips curved, not quite a smile. "Someone had to."

He slammed the papers down. "What are you doing with these."

"Making sure you don't sink us both," she said.

"You mean selling me."

"You already sold yourself," she said.

He slept on the floor that night. She stayed on the bed, her back to him, phone screen glowing until dawn.

The flat felt smaller, tighter, the walls holding too much. He stared at the ceiling until morning, knowing the betrayal had already begun, whether or not she admitted it.

17

The Watcher Steps In

The first sign was small. A cigarette butt on their balcony ledge. Neither of them smoked there.

He picked it up with two fingers, stared at the lipstick smear on the filter, then at her. She raised her eyebrows.

"Not mine," she said.

He dropped it in the ashtray. Neither spoke more.

Two days later, the lock turned rough again. He had oiled it last week, could still smell the faint grease. Now the bolt caught halfway, then gave with a sound that wasn't right.

Inside, nothing was missing. But something had shifted.

She noticed it too. She opened the cupboard, looked at the way clothes leaned, the angle of hangers. She shut it, eyes narrow.

"They've been in here," she said.

"Who."

"Not us."

That night, he woke to the sound of a chair scraping. He sat up, heart thudding. The room was dark, but not empty. He felt it. The presence of someone watching.

He stood, hand reaching for the switch. The bulb flared, yellow, revealing nothing. The chair was where it had always been. She stirred on the bed, eyes opening slow.

"What is it."

"Someone was here."

"You're dreaming."

"No."

She sat up, looked at the chair, then at him. "Then they still are."

The next morning, they found the envelope. Slid under the door, no address, no seal. Inside: photographs.

Not of the body on the balcony. Of them.

Smoking at the window. Arguing in the kitchen. Her leaning over him on the sofa. His hand on the drawer.

Each one grainy, taken from an angle that belonged nowhere inside the flat.

She spread them across the table, cigarette trembling between her fingers.

"They're in the walls," she said.

He stared at his own face on paper, caught mid-gesture, unaware. "How long."

"Since before we met," she said.

He took the photos, shoved them back into the envelope, stuffed it in the drawer. His hand shook when he closed it.

"We go to the police," he said.

She laughed, sharp. "We're already suspects. You want to hand them proof?"

"Then what."

She leaned forward, scar catching light. "We wait."

"For what."

"For them to show."

That evening, the doorbell rang. Not a neighbour's knock, not the police's flat rap. A single press, long, patient.

She froze in the kitchen. He stood in the hall, staring at the door.

"Don't," she whispered.

He opened it anyway.

A man stood there. Not polished shoes. Not police. Ordinary clothes, plain face, camera strap around his neck.

"You should close your curtains," the man said. His voice was low, even.

"Who are you."

The man smiled faintly. "Someone who knows more than your neighbours."

She stepped into the hall. "You've been watching us."

"Yes."

"Why."

"Because it matters."

"To who."

"To me."

He tried to shut the door. The man put his hand out, calm, not forcing, just stopping.

"You can close it," the man said. "But I'll still see."

She lit a cigarette, inhaled deep, exhaled slow. "What do you want."

The man's eyes flicked to her, then back to him. "The truth."

"We don't have it," she said.

"You do," the man said. "You just don't know which one to keep."

The man left as quietly as he arrived. No threats. No promises. Just presence.

When the door clicked shut, she leaned against it, cigarette burning to her fingers.

"He's not police," she said.

"No," he said.

"He's worse."

[Watcher's Note | Day 26]

Direct contact initiated.
Subjects visibly destabilized.
Reaction patterns: denial, fear, partial aggression.
Apartment compromised. Continue phase advancement.

The following night, another envelope appeared. This time it carried only one photograph.

Her. Sleeping.

Taken from inside the bedroom.

She stared at it until her hands shook. He snatched it away, shoved it back in the envelope, threw it in the drawer.

She grabbed his wrist. "Don't bury it."

"What else."

"Burn it."

He lit a match, held the flame to the corner. The paper curled, blackened, turned to ash. They watched it fall in fragments into the tray.

But the image remained in her head. In his too.

They slept with the lights on. The fan turned overhead, ticking every fourth round, as if marking them.

She whispered into the dark, "He knows everything."

He whispered back, "So do we."

Neither believed the other.

18

The Crime Revisited

The stain was still there. Faded, scrubbed, bleached, but present.

She stood at the window, cigarette between her fingers, eyes fixed on the opposite slab. Morning light didn't erase it. If anything, it made the mark sharper, a ghost refusing to leave.

"She's still down there," she said.

He glanced up from the table, where bills lay scattered like fallen leaves. "Don't start."

"She is." She exhaled smoke, thin, steady. "We've been pretending it was just noise. A scream. A body. But she didn't leave."

He rubbed his temples. "She's in the ground."

"She's in this flat," she said.

That evening the police called them again.

Not a station summons. A request. Meet at the building opposite. Walk the balcony. Revisit the scene.

The watchman let them through the gate. The building smelled of damp stone and incense. Neighbours' eyes followed them up the stairs, whispering low.

On the third floor, yellow tape sagged across the doorway. A constable lifted it, motioned them inside.

The flat was bare. Curtains pulled down. Furniture pushed against walls. Only the balcony remained as it had been, iron railing, chipped cement, faint stain of blood darkened into the surface.

She stepped out first, lit a cigarette. The flame shook in the breeze. He followed, reluctant, hands in his pockets.

The officer with the square face stood behind them, file in hand.

"Show me," the officer said.

"Show what," he asked.

"What you saw," the officer said.

He gestured to the slab below. "She was there."

"How," the officer asked.

"Fell," he said.

"Jumped," she said at the same time.

The officer looked at both. Wrote nothing.

"Again," the officer said.

He closed his eyes. "Scream. Then silence. Then the body."

"From where," the officer said.

He pointed to the railing.

"From whom," the officer said.

"Not us," he whispered.

The officer turned to her. "Your version."

She flicked ash over the rail. "She was pushed."

"By who."

"Someone she knew."

The officer's eyes narrowed. "You."

Her gaze didn't flinch. "Not me."

The officer turned to him. "Not him?"

She smiled faintly. "Not yet."

When they left, the officer's voice followed. "Truth always leaves stains."

They walked home in silence. The street felt longer. Every face they passed seemed to watch.

At night, he dreamed of her scream again. But this time, it was her face he saw falling. Not the stranger's. Hers.

He woke with sweat damp on his neck, the sheet tangled around his legs. She lay beside him, eyes open.

"You heard it too," she said.

"I dreamed."

She shook her head. "We're both awake."

[Watcher's Note | Day 28]

Subjects revisited crime scene under supervision.
Accounts contradictory: Subject M claims fall, Subject F claims push.
Observation: high stress, mutual distrust.
Notable: Subject F exhibited unusual composure. Subject M avoidance behaviour.
Stain persists. Symbolic weight observed.

The next day, another envelope arrived. This one contained a single photograph.

Not of them. Of the dead woman.

Alive. On the balcony. Leaning against the rail, cigarette between fingers. Smiling.

The photo was time-stamped. One day before the fall.

He stared at it. "Where did this come from."

She took it from him, studied it. "Not from us."

"You recognize her?"

Her thumb traced the edge. "Maybe."

"Maybe who."

"Someone I almost was," she said.

That evening, he confronted her.

"You knew her."

"She worked in my office," she said.

"You told the police you didn't."

"I told them what they wanted."

"You lied."

She lit a cigarette. "We both did."

"Why didn't you tell me."

"Because you would have asked why she was on your balcony."

He froze. "My balcony?"

She looked at him steadily. "That's what I asked myself when I saw her picture."

He couldn't breathe. He paced the flat, pulled at his hair, sat, stood again.

"You think I..."

"I think we don't know what we did that night," she said.

The next morning, the watchman avoided their eyes. The neighbours whispered louder. The flat grew tighter. The stain across the street grew darker.

She stood at the window, smoke curling. "We're in the wrong story," she said.

He turned, voice breaking. "No. We're the story."

19

No Exit

The flat had grown smaller. Not in square feet, but in possibility. Every door felt heavier, every window a mirror instead of a view.

She stood at the sink rinsing a cup that was already clean. He sat at the table with an unlit cigarette, staring at the wall. The fan ticked every fourth turn, keeping count.

"They'll come again," she said.

"They always do."

"Not just the police."

He looked up. "Then who."

She dried the cup slowly, deliberately, as though she were teaching him patience. "The one who knocks without needing to."

That evening, the doorbell rang.

They froze. Not a neighbour's tap. Not the police's rap. The long, steady press.

She put the cup down. He stood, moved to the door, peered through the peephole.

Empty corridor.

He opened anyway.

An envelope on the floor. No one in sight.

Inside: a photograph.

Them. Asleep. His arm over her waist. Her head on his shoulder. Taken from above.

He stared until the edges cut his fingers. She leaned against the doorframe, smoke curling from her lips.

"He was in the room," she said.

He dropped the photo in the ashtray, lit it, watched it curl and blacken. The smoke that rose didn't leave. It clung.

The next morning, they tried to leave.

He packed a small bag, she grabbed her jacket. They moved quietly, as if the flat itself might protest.

Downstairs, the watchman stopped them. His voice polite, his stance firm.

"Police orders," he said. "No one leaves until further notice."

"Since when," he asked.

"Since you became the notice," the watchman said.

They turned back. The corridor felt longer, the stairs steeper. The flat, when they returned, was waiting like a cage.

In the afternoon, the phone rang. Not hers. Not his. The landline neither of them used.

He picked it up.

A voice: calm, steady. "You cannot leave."

"Who is this."

"You know."

"What do you want."

"Nothing," the voice said. "Just to watch."

Click.

The line went dead.

He stared at the receiver, knuckles white. She stood at the door, eyes narrow. "So now he talks."

That night they argued again. Not about lies, not about debts. About the simple fact of air.

"You smoke too much," he said.

"You breathe too loud," she said.

"You check the window every five minutes."

"You check the drawer every two."

They stood across the room from each other, two silhouettes in the thin light, both too tired to leave, too restless to stay.

Finally, she said, "We're not fighting each other anymore. We're fighting the walls."

[Watcher's Note | Day 31]

Subjects attempted exit. Prevented by external directive.
Contact initiated via landline.
Subjects exhibiting confinement stress.
Apartment integrity: maintained. No exit possible.

By the third day of confinement, the neighbours had turned hostile. Notes slid under their door: *Murderers. Leave. We see you.*

She gathered them in a pile, burned them one by one in the sink. He watched, silent, until the smoke alarm buzzed weakly and then died.

"They want us gone," he said.

"They want us guilty," she replied.

The fourth day, food delivery stopped. The watchman refused packages. The grocer said no account existed.

"We're being erased," he said.

"Not erased," she said. "Pinned."

On the fifth night, the power cut. The flat plunged into black.

He lit a match. The flame barely reached the walls. She lit a cigarette from the same flame, inhaled, exhaled.

"You ever feel like this place is breathing," she said.

He didn't answer. He pressed his ear to the wall instead.

Footsteps. Inside the plaster.

He pulled back, heart hammering. She tilted her head, listening. The fan clicked once in the dark, though the power was gone.

In the morning, the lights returned. The fan spun as if nothing had happened. The matchbox was empty.

On the table lay another photograph.

Not delivered. Already there.

Them. At the sink. Burning the notes.

She looked at him. He looked at her. Neither spoke.

The flat was no longer just a witness. It had become the evidence.

20

Secrets Surface Again

The room smelled of smoke and damp clothes. They had stopped opening windows; outside meant eyes Inside meant breathing the same air until it grew stale, heavy.

She sat on the sofa with her knees drawn up, cigarette balanced on the edge of the ashtray. He stood by the sink, staring at his reflection in the steel tap.

Neither had spoken for hours.

Finally, she said, "We should talk."

He turned. "We do nothing else."

"No," she said. "We circle. We don't land."

She reached for the cigarette, dragged once, exhaled. "Her name was Anarya."

The sound of it filled the room like a crack.

He stayed still.

"She worked in my office," she went on. "Not on my team. But close enough to know things. She knew who I was with. She knew who I wasn't."

"And you never told me," he said.

"You never asked."

He moved closer, voice tight. "You lied to the police."

She met his eyes. "So did you."

He sat on the chair across from her. His hands trembled against his knees. "Why hide her name."

"She was having an affair," she said. "With my boss."

"Your boss."

"The one I was with before you."

He stared. The words rearranged his sense of her. "She knew."

"She threatened to tell his wife. He threatened to cut her out. She liked pressure. She liked seeing people squirm. Then she fell."

"Or was pushed," he said.

Her silence was answer enough.

His turn came slow. He leaned back, let the words crawl out. "I owe twelve lakhs."

She blinked once, slow. "Not three."

"Three is what I told you. Three is what I tell myself so I can still breathe."

"Who do you owe."

132

"Everyone who doesn't ask for receipts," he said. "Small loans. Big loans. One man with polished shoes who smiles too much."

Her cigarette burned to the filter. She stubbed it out hard. "You think they want their money. They don't. They want you broken."

"And now you too."

Silence thickened. The fan ticked, marking their lies turned truths.

She spoke again. "That photograph of you. With her. It wasn't old."

His eyes snapped up. "What are you saying."

"She showed it to me once. Smiled when she said you'd come back around."

He shook his head. "No."

"She had proof," she said.

He slammed the table. "She had lies."

The sound echoed. Neighbours stirred. A door shut hard down the corridor.

He stood, pacing, pulling at his hair. "You think I killed her."

"I think you didn't have to."

"What does that mean."

"Some people fall on their own," she said.

That night they lay apart. The bed a line of cold between them.

He whispered into the dark, "You think I could push her."

She whispered back, "You think I could."

Neither answered.

[Watcher's Note | Day 34]

Subject F disclosure: victim identified as Ananya, coworker, affair with superior.
Subject M disclosure: debt liability confirmed, twelve lakhs.
Interaction: heightened mistrust, mutual accusations.
Probability of fracture: critical.

The next morning, another envelope under the door. Inside: a page torn from a notebook.

In handwriting neither of them recognized:

"One of you pushed. One of you paid. Both of you lie."

She read it twice, then passed it to him. He folded it, placed it in the drawer with the photograph. His hand lingered on the wood.

"No more secrets," he said.

"No more lies," she said.

But the room itself didn't believe them.

21

The Betrayal Deepens

The note stayed in the drawer with the photograph. *One of you pushed. One of you paid. Both of you lie.*

They moved around it as if the wood were hot.

She made tea. He stood by the sink and watched the kettle cloud the air. The fan ticked every fourth turn. The sound had begun to feel like a metronome for decisions.

"You sleep at all," she asked.

"No."

"Good," she said. "You think clearer when you are tired."

He looked at her without answering. He couldn't tell if she was joking.

They sipped in silence. He counted the seconds between swallows. She watched the window, the curtain breathing in a draft they could not feel.

He said, "We should clear everything."

She said, "We should not clear anything. Clearing leaves marks."

He set his cup down. "I will go downstairs. Groceries."

"We are on a list," she said. "The watchman will stop you."

"I will ask him anyway."

She watched him pick up the keys. "Ask politely. Men with lists prefer polite."

He nodded. He did not take the bag.

Downstairs the watchman looked up, eyes tired, fingers on the register. "Orders are orders," he said, light, as if repeating a nursery rhyme.

"I only need bread," he said.

"Someone will send," the watchman said. "You stay."

He thanked him. He did not return to the flat. He stood in the stairwell with his back to the cool wall and waited. After a minute a shape detached itself from the shadow near the service lift.

Polished shoes.

"You are restless," the man said.

"You said three days. Today is three."

The man's hands were soft, nails trimmed. "Then today is expensive."

"I do not have it."

"You never do."

He swallowed. "I can open a door."

The man tilted his head. "A door to what."

"To things you can carry."

"Jewellery," the man asked.

"No."

"Then not interesting."

"Laptops. Documents. An envelope with numbers you like. And a person who will not scream."

The man's gaze sharpened. "Whose person."

"Mine," he said. "For now."

Polished shoes smiled without showing teeth. "Leave the bolt soft," he said. "Leave at eleven. Come back at twelve. If there is trouble, you never saw me."

He nodded. He felt sick.

"Say it," the man said.

"What."

"Say you never saw me," the man said, smiling. "Practice."

He said it. The man's eyes stayed flat. Then the man melted back to the service lift and was gone.

He climbed slowly. Each landing felt steeper than the last. At his floor he stopped, hand on the rail. He could hear the fan ticking through the door. It matched his pulse.

He knocked softly and let himself in.

She was by the window with a cigarette and her phone. She did not ask why it took so long. She did not look at the time.

An envelope lay under the door when she woke from a nap she had not meant to take. No noise, just paper on the floor.

She did not open it immediately. She placed it on the table, lit a cigarette, and stared. He was in the bathroom running the tap hard as if water could erase something.

When he came out, she slid the envelope toward him. "Your admirer," she said.

He shook his head. "Yours."

She opened it.

A single photograph. The stairwell from above. A man with polished shoes near the service lift. Another figure in shadow. The angle made faces useless, but the shape of a hand was clear on the rail. His hand. The scar on one knuckle like a comma.

She looked up. He looked at the sink.

"Groceries," she said.

He did not answer.

She put the photograph back in the envelope and slid it under the drawer, not into it. The drawer did not deserve it.

"Walk with me," she said.

"We cannot leave."

"We do not have to," she said. "Roof."

He nodded. They went without cups or cigarettes. The stairs to the terrace smelled of dust and old rain. The lock on the door was weak, an old hasp with a fresh chain that someone had threaded wrong. She touched the knot with two fingers and smiled.

"You learn where buildings lie," she said.

They stepped onto the roof. The city lay flat and hot, balconies open like mouths on every side. A water tank squatted in the corner. Laundry lines stretched with no laundry.

She stood behind the tank and lit a cigarette with two hands to hide the flame. He stood beside the parapet with his palms on the rough edge and looked down. Opposite, the stain on the slab was almost gone in the light. Almost.

"I want to make a trade," she said.

"With whom."

"The one who knocks without needing to."

140

"Why."

"Because he is already inside."

He said nothing.

"If I give him something, he will choose a side," she said.

"Which side."

"Mine," she said, as if that should be obvious.

"What do you give him."

She took a slip of paper from her pocket and held it up. A number. A login. The handwriting was his. The copy she had made the day he wrote it at the station for the officer with the square face. She had traced the digits there on the desk, eyes down, shoulder to shoulder.

"Insurance," she said.

"You cannot keep handing me to people," he said.

"Then start holding yourself," she said, and put the paper away.

They went back down. She closed the terrace door the way she had found it, wrong chain, right lie.

At six, the landline rang.

She picked it up this time. "Yes."

"You have something," the voice said.

"You already know," she said.

"You want what," the voice asked.

"Choice," she said.

"You have it," the voice said. "For now."

"Meet," she said.

"Where."

"Here," she said. "On the roof. Ten."

The line clicked.

He watched her hang up. "You told him to come."

"He was coming anyway," she said. "At least now he will meet me first."

"You think he keeps that promise."

"I think he likes to be asked," she said.

He looked at the clock. Four hours until ten. He wanted to ask what she planned to say. He wanted to tell her not to go. He wanted to pull the chain right on the terrace door and lock the rest of his life behind it. He went to the kitchen and washed a clean cup.

At nine he changed his shirt. She changed nothing. She tied her hair and put on his jacket. It looked better on her.

They went out at five to ten. The corridor was empty. The watchman was not at his post. The building had decided to hold its breath.

On the terrace the air felt different. Not cool. Not soft. Just aware. The water tank hummed quietly as if keeping something for later.

He stood by the door. She moved to the shadow behind the tank. At ten a figure stepped out near the parapet. Not polished shoes. Camera strap.

"You should not smoke," he said.

She ignored it. "You came."

"I always do," he said.

She held up the slip of paper. "You want it."

He tilted his head. "I already have it."

She smiled. "Then you came for me."

He did not smile back. "You wanted to talk."

She stepped closer, cigarette between fingers, the ash ready to drop. "You will keep him out of the way tonight," she said. "And you will leave my name off your file when this goes to whoever you serve."

"I serve the same thing everyone does," he said. "Myself."

"Good," she said. "Then price matters."

"What is it."

She looked past him at the city, then back. "Not money. Not yet. I want you at the door when men with polished shoes come. I want you to make them feel seen."

"That is easy," he said.

"And you hand me copies of the photographs you have of the balcony," she said. "All of them."

"You will burn them," he said.

"Maybe," she said. "Maybe I hang one on my wall to remember who I was."

He watched her. He was good at that. "And for this," he asked, "what do I get."

"You get the thing you always wanted," she said. "The true story."

He did not laugh. He nodded instead, once, small. "At eleven," he said, "he will leave the bolt soft."

She did not look surprised. "You already knew," she said.

"I know most things too late," he said. "Tonight, I know early."

"Do you help him," she asked.

"I help the story," he said. "He is part of it."

She dropped the ash and crushed it with her shoe. "Then watch closely," she said. "I am writing the next page."

He faded back, the camera strap dark against his shirt. He did not thank her. He did not promise anything. He left with the shape of a man who never leaves.

She and he walked down without speaking. At the door to the flat she touched the lock. The bolt moved slowly, then gave. He did not need to force it.

"You are sure," he said.

"No," she said. "That is why it will work."

They did not turn on the big light. The table lamp gave the room a small circle to stand inside. She placed the drawer keys on the table. He left his wallet next to them. They sat on opposite sides of the circle and watched the seconds bleed to eleven.

At eleven he stood. "I will go," he said. "Walk the corridor. Look like I am tired of walls."

"You are," she said.

He opened the door, stepped out, and closed it softly. His footsteps faded toward the lift.

She counted to sixty. On sixty-one she moved.

She took the slip of paper with his numbers and slid it into the toothbrush mug where she kept hers. She took the envelope with the photograph and the note and placed it on the bed. She took the small pin she used for earrings and slipped it under the rubber mat by the door so the latch would not sit right when it closed.

She turned off the lamp. The room settled around her. The fan clicked on its fourth turn as if raising a hand to say present.

Keys moved in a lock. Not hers. Not his.

The door opened an inch, then an inch more. A shadow slipped through without breath.

She stayed in the dark and let it move. It was heavier than the watcher and lighter than the police. It smelled of cologne and soap and money counted often. It moved like a person who believed rooms owed him.

"Hello," she said, low.

The shadow stopped. A lighter flared, quick, then died. A face made itself for a second and then went away.

"You are alone," the voice said.

"For now," she said.

"You left it soft," the voice said, amused. "Good girl."

She let the sentence sit without meaning. "Take what you came for."

"What I came for is not paper," he said.

"Then take what you expect," she said. "Laptop. Passport. Photographs. I left your favourites on top."

The man chuckled without sound. "You have learned my favourites."

"I learn fast," she said.

The shape moved to the table, then to the drawer. Wood slid. Paper touched paper. A small rustle like a mouse crossing a newspaper. He whistled under his breath as if surprised by how easy life could be.

She leaned against the wall and listened. She could hear the chain shift on the terrace in the wind. She could hear the lift rise and stop and then not open. She could hear the camera on a strap somewhere beyond the corridor finding a place to see.

"Do not take the note," she said.

He stopped. "What note."

"The one that says we both lie," she said. "Leave it. It belongs to us."

He laughed a little, for real this time. "You are sentimental."

"I am tired," she said.

He went back to work. A zipper. The click of a passport case. A drawer shut too hard. The tiny, familiar snick of a SIM tray opening. He was fast. He had done this before. He would do it again.

Footsteps in the corridor. Slow. Measured. A second shadow at the door. The cologne man did not hear it.

He had the sound of victory in his ears and it made him deaf.

The second shadow did not enter. It stayed at the edge the way surf holds itself on a beach until the next push. The camera strap touched wood. A breath moved air.

"Time," she said.

Polished shoes looked up. "What."

"Time," she said again, louder.

And then the light came on.

Not the big light. The camera light. A small square of hard white that flattened faces and lifted truth out of corners. The second shadow stepped into it and the lens made a soft motor sound that said yes.

Polished shoes froze with the passport in his hand and the photograph half in his pocket. The camera saw everything and forgave nothing. She stood with her arms folded and watched.

"You," polished shoes said.

"You," the watcher said, pleasant as tea.

The camera kept its small sound. The room became a file.

He backed toward the door, the passport still in his hand. The watcher did not move, but the light made the room narrow.

"You do not want this," polished shoes said.

"I want exactly this," the watcher said.

"You cannot show it," polished shoes said. "You have no right."

The watcher's smile did not travel to his eyes. "I never asked for rights."

Polished shoes put the passport down very slowly, as if that would reverse time. He placed the photograph gently beside it. Then he stepped toward the door.

The pin under the mat caught his heel. He stumbled. The camera followed with a small step. He caught himself on the jamb and breathed once as if he had been underwater.

"You will regret this," polished shoes said.

"I regret many things," the watcher said. "Not this."

Polished shoes left without hurry. The watcher stayed. He turned the camera to her. He turned the light off. The room softened a fraction.

"You invited him," he said.

"Someone had to," she said.

He nodded. "He will come back with friends."

"I have none," she said.

"You do now," he said. He did not say which kind. He did not need to.

The door opened again. He returned.

Not polished shoes. Him.

He stopped in the frame and looked at the table and looked at the camera and looked at her. His face did not break. It set.

"What did you do," he asked.

"What did you plan," she asked.

They held the questions between them like knives at each other's throats and waited to see who would cut first.

The watcher looked from one to the other and then stepped back so they filled the picture without him.

"Finish your scene," he said, almost kind.

[Watcher's Note | Day 35]

Interior event recorded.
Subject M vacated premises at 23:00 hrs.
Bolt left unsecured.
Male associate entered at 23:11 hrs.
Attempted removal of documents and devices.
Secondary party present with recording apparatus. Visual evidence captured.
Subject F initiated contact, controlled environment.
Outcome: extraction aborted. Escalation expected.

He closed the door behind him and left them with the note and the photograph and the passport and the drawer that had learned how to open itself.

He spoke first. "I asked him to come."

"I know," she said.

"You set him up."

"I know," she said.

He took one step into the circle of lamplight. "Did you do it for me," he asked.

She took one step too. "I did it so this room does not eat us."

He looked at the table. He looked at the door. He looked at her.

"We are past saving," he said.

"We are past hiding," she said.

They stood in the small light with all the doors soft and all the eyes open and felt the story tighten around them.

He reached for the drawer and did not open it.

She reached for her cigarette and did not light it.

Outside, the lift rose and stopped and opened to no one. Inside, the fan ticked and ticked and did not miss.

22

Escalation

Morning crawled in through the curtains, pale and unforgiving. Neither of them had slept.

She sat cross-legged on the sofa, smoking, eyes on the floor. He stood by the table, staring at the drawer without touching it. The fan ticked overhead, steady as a pulse.

At eight sharp, the bell rang.

They froze.

"Not him," she whispered.

He opened anyway.

Two police officers stood there. Square-face in front, younger one behind with a file under his arm. Their expressions were calm, the calm of people who already knew the answers.

"Come," square-face said.

At the station, they were separated again. The rooms smelled of disinfectant and sweat. This time the questions were different.

"Who is Ananya," square-face asked him.

He swallowed. "A neighbour."

The officer opened a folder, slid a photograph across the table. Her. Laughing, cigarette in hand, scar catching light.

"She worked in your girlfriend's office," the officer said. "She told us yesterday."

His throat went dry. "I didn't know."

"You knew enough to keep a photograph," the officer said. "Drawer. Under the bills."

He said nothing.

"You think drawers don't talk," the officer asked.

In the other room, the lady officer with the braid leaned over the table.

"Where were you the night of her fall," she asked her.

"Here," she said.

"Not on the balcony."

"No."

The officer slid her phone across. On the screen: a video, grainy. A figure leaning out from their flat, a cigarette glowing, a face caught half in shadow. Her scar glinting faintly.

"That is you," the officer said.

She looked at the screen, exhaled smoke. "That is a shadow," she said.

The officer's pen didn't move. "Shadows don't smoke," she said.

By noon they were back in the flat. Released, but not free.

He dropped onto the chair, head in his hands. She went to the window, lit another cigarette.

"They know," he said.

"They always did," she said.

At four, the landline rang.

He picked up. Silence first. Then a voice, smooth, steady.

"You embarrassed him," the voice said.

"Who."

"You know who. He does not forgive."

The line clicked dead.

He stood with the receiver in his hand. She watched, smoke curling.

"What did he say," she asked.

"That we started a war."

She smiled faintly. "Good."

That night, footsteps in the corridor. Slow, deliberate. A scrape against the door, then silence.

She reached for the drawer. He stopped her hand. "Don't."

"Why not."

"Because they want us to."

They sat in the dark, waiting, until the footsteps faded.

```
[Watcher's Note | Day 37]

Police re-interrogation: contradictions
logged.
Subject F identified in video footage.
Subject M confronted with drawer
photograph.
Debt associate retaliatory intent
confirmed.
Apartment under heightened surveillance.
Assessment: escalation phase active.
```

The next morning, the watchman wouldn't meet their eyes. He handed them a folded paper instead.

Written in neat block letters: "Leave before midnight. Or you will be carried out."

She read it, folded it once, set it on the table.

He stared at it. "We can't leave."

"We were never going to," she said.

At dusk, the power cut again. This time, the corridor lights died too. They lit candles, shadows stretching across the walls. The flat felt alive, the walls breathing, listening.

She whispered, "We are not trapped. We are cornered. That's different."

"How," he asked.

"In a corner, you still get to choose which way to strike," she said.

At midnight, the doorbell rang. Not long, not patient. Three sharp presses.

She crushed her cigarette, stood. He stayed seated.

"You are expecting someone," he asked.

"Yes," she said.

The bolt slid back before he could stop her.

The door opened.

And the flat held its breath.

23

Through the Ashes

The door opened.

A thin slice of corridor light cut the room. She did not move. He stood, half-turned, one hand on the back of the chair as if a piece of furniture could help.

Two men entered. Not the watcher. Not police. The first wore a shirt too clean for midnight. The second carried a length of pipe wrapped with tape.

They closed the door gently. The corridor light vanished. The room breathed once and went still.

"Good evening," the clean shirt said.

No one answered.

He shifted his weight. The pipe tilted toward his knees. He stilled.

"You embarrass a client," the clean shirt said, voice easy. "He misplaces his manners."

She lit a cigarette. The flame showed the scar on her lip, then hid it. "He misplaces more than that," she said.

The clean shirt smiled without warmth. "Money first. Manners after."

He reached toward the drawer. She spoke fast. "Don't."

The pipe tapped the table, soft. "Open," the clean shirt said.

He slid the drawer out. Papers. The photograph. The note. The clean shirt looked like a man admiring a dessert before tasting it.

"Passport," he said.

"In the back," she said.

He shot her a look. She did not return it. She watched the lighter's flame die and left the cigarette burning.

The clean shirt's fingers were careful. He lifted the passport, flipped, checked. He placed it on the table, then nudged the photograph with one knuckle.

"You keep souvenirs," he said.

"Throw it," she said.

He didn't. He let the pipe man do the lazy work. The pipe folded a page. The photograph bent, then lay flat again, a crease like a vein through the middle.

"Phones," the clean shirt said.

"With police," he said.

"Everything else," the clean shirt said.

He kept his eyes on the table. She crossed to the sink, opened the tap until water ran hard. The sound filled the edges of the room. She turned it off. The silence after was heavier.

"You had three days," the clean shirt said. "You used them badly."

He took a half-step forward. The pipe lifted. He stopped.

"Sit," the clean shirt told him.

He sat.

"You," the clean shirt told her.

She leaned against the counter. "Standing is honest," she said.

"Honesty bores me," he said.

"Then talk to yourself," she said.

The pipe moved fast. The sound of metal on wood. The chair shuddered under him. He did not fall. He kept his hands where they were, palms up, empty.

The clean shirt drifted toward the window and pulled the curtain back two fingers' width. The city's dark pressed through. "Nice view," he said. "People watch you. They all do."

"Some of us watch back," she said.

He let the curtain fall. "You will pack a bag in the morning," he said, as if they had agreed. "You will come to a place where lists are short. You will sign some things. You will sell some things. Then you will learn to sleep early."

"No," she said.

He turned to her, mild, surprised to find a word that refused to move. "No?"

"No," she repeated.

The pipe man shifted his weight. The tape crackled under his fingers.

The clean shirt spread his hands. "Talk to her," he told the man on the chair, as if he were not present.

He did not. He looked at the cigarette in her hand and the tiny ash trembling at the tip.

The clean shirt picked up the note from the drawer and read it out loud, pleasant as a radio host. "One of you pushed. One of you paid. Both of you lie." He replaced it delicately. "Poetry," he said. "People like stories that rhyme."

"Then go buy one," she said.

The pipe came down. It hit the edge of the table and glanced into his forearm. A dull blow, not sharp, enough to make the arm dead for a second. He hissed, breath short. The pipe lifted again, slower this time, choosing.

"Stop," she said.

It stopped.

The clean shirt's eyes lifted, amused. "You care," he said.

"I hate cleaning blood," she said.

He considered this, and for the first time his smile almost reached his eyes. "Reasonable," he said. "Then make a call. Someone else will clean."

"Who," she asked.

"You already have him," the clean shirt said. "The man with the camera."

She tilted her head. "You know him."

"We all do," the clean shirt said. "We send him news when we want to be good, and dirt when we want to be monsters."

"You want to be both," she said.

"I want to be paid," he said.

She took a long drag and let the smoke roll from her mouth slow. "He is not yours," she said.

"He is not yours either," the clean shirt said. "He is the story."

The pipe touched the table again. A gentle knock, like a reminder. The room heard it.

He shifted his weight on the chair. The wood creaked. He felt the bruise on his forearm begin to throb with its own small heart. He thought of the roof, of the chain looped wrong, of the camera light like a square of hard morning. He thought of the stain across the way, how it stayed even when scrubbed.

She flicked ash into the sink. "You will take the passport," she said. "You will take a laptop. You will take the envelope in the back with photocopies you cannot use but will show to your friends. Then you leave."

The clean shirt tilted his head. "And you keep what," he asked.

"My name," she said.

He laughed softly. "Names are cheap."

"Not this one," she said.

The pipe lifted, uncertain, then lowered. The clean shirt tapped the passport with two fingers, a small drumbeat, a decision forming. "Maybe," he said.

The landline rang.

No one moved.

It rang again. Four times. Five. It stopped.

A second later, the doorbell sounded. One press. Long. Patient.

The clean shirt's eyes flicked to the door and back. "You have many friends," he said.

"We have many watchers," she said.

"Let him in," the clean shirt told the pipe man, as if hosts still existed here.

The pipe man slid the bolt back. The door opened a hand's width. Light from the corridor slipped in thin and bright.

No one stood there.

The pipe man looked left, then right, then out. He leaned a step into the corridor.

The camera light clicked on.

Soft. Square. Hard.

It ate the shadows. It drew lines around faces. It made the clean shirt less clean.

The watcher stepped into the rectangle, not in a hurry. The pipe man took a step back without meaning to. The door shut behind him with a small, automatic sound.

"You again," the clean shirt said.

"Still," the watcher said.

"This is private," the clean shirt said.

The watcher looked around the room. The burnt edges of old paper in the ashtray. The open drawer with its careful mess. The way the fan's click timed the air. He raised the camera and let it see.

The pipe lifted, half at the camera, half at the man behind it. The watcher did not shift. The light did not blink.

"You will put that down," the clean shirt said.

"I will not," the watcher said.

"Then you will leave," the clean shirt said.

"I will not," the watcher said again.

The pipe man moved. Quick this time, like a choice finally chosen. The watcher stepped sideways, small, as if avoiding a puddle. The pipe hit the door frame. The sound was dull, humiliating. The camera did not shake.

"Careful," the watcher said. "You will hurt your house."

The clean shirt breathed out through his nose. "Enough," he said, not loud. He pinched the passport between two fingers again, then placed it back, then moved his hand away. He was making shapes with his choices now.

"You have what you want," she said.

"I do not," he said.

"You have a way out," she said.

He considered the door, the camera, the pipe, the chair, the man, the woman, the drawer that would one day be empty. He smiled without his eyes. "I have a way through," he said.

He snatched the note instead of the passport. The paper that had lived with them like a curse. *One of you pushed. One of you paid. Both of you lie.* He folded it once and slipped it into his shirt pocket.

"That is mine," she said.

"It is everyone's," he said.

The pipe man grabbed the laptop. A cable tore. The plug sparked once and went quiet. He slung it under his arm like a child.

The watcher lowered the camera an inch. "Say thank you," he told the clean shirt.

"For what," the clean shirt asked.

"For leaving with less," the watcher said.

The clean shirt gave a little bow to no one. "Thank you," he said, and it sounded almost beautiful. He nodded to the pipe man. They moved to the door.

The door did not open.

The pin under the mat had found its moment. The latch kissed the frame and held. The pipe man pulled. The latch held again.

The clean shirt looked down, bent, found the edge of the rubber with two fingers, lifted, smiled. "Children," he said, amused. He flicked the pin away and opened the door like history.

They stepped into the corridor. The watcher followed them to the threshold, then stopped. The light stayed on their backs until they turned the corner. Footsteps faded. Silence returned by habit.

He exhaled shakily. She set the cigarette down and watched it burn to the filter.

The watcher lowered the camera fully now. He looked at the table, the open drawer, the passport where it sat, the envelope half-emptied, the laptop gone.

"You will call the police," he said.

"They will call us," she said.

"They will call both," he said. "They enjoy balance."

He turned the camera to her for a moment longer, brief, precise, as if taking a measurement. He nodded once, a small acknowledgment of something that had no word.

"Keep your curtains closed," he said.

"You like them open," she said.

"I like them honest," he said.

He left. The rectangle of light retreated into the corridor and went out. The door shut with the finality of a thing that had learned how to do it properly.

They stood still until the fan's click made them move.

He crossed to the table. He picked up the passport and held it to his chest for a second, the way a person checks his own pulse. He placed it back and shut the drawer.

She went to the sink, turned the tap, then turned it off again. She touched the ashtray. The cigarette had gone out. She ground it further into grey.

He looked at his forearm. The bruise was coming up now, a blue under the skin like a river line on a map. He flexed his fingers. They worked.

She picked up the lighter and the envelope with the torn edge. She struck the wheel. The flame caught. She held it under the photograph lying bent on the table. It curled slow. The crease vanished in heat. The image darkened, then flaked into black. She dropped the ashes into the tray. The air shifted, warm and bitter.

"Stop," he said.

"Why," she asked.

"It will bring them," he said.

"They are already here," she said.

They burned the rest. Not everything. Not the passport. Not the papers that would be asked for later.

167

Only the things that told a story to strangers. The room filled with a thin veil. It smelled like old secrets and bad tea.

Neighbours stirred behind walls. A door opened. Someone coughed. Someone laughed once, sharp.

He ran the exhaust fan. It whined. It did nothing.

They stood over the sink, watching grey gather.

A knock. Not a bell. A flat, official knock. Three times. Then again.

They did not speak.

He opened the door.

Square-face stood there with the lady officer. No file this time. No biscuits. Their expressions were tired and clear.

"Your neighbours called," square-face said. He looked past them into the smoke. "So did someone else."

The lady officer's eyes went to the table, to the drawer shut too neatly, to the small black pile in the ashtray. "What burned," she asked.

"Bad writing," she said.

"Where is the laptop," the officer asked.

"Stolen," he said.

Square-face walked in as if the room belonged to him. He touched nothing. He looked at the skirting, at the door frame, at the p_n on the floor kicked under the shoe rack, at the tiny laughter line the pipe had left at the edge of the table.

He nodded once, to himself. "You will come," he said.

"For what," she asked.

"For the part where you tell me what you did," he said.

"We already told you," she said.

The lady officer took out her phone, turned the screen to them. A clip. Fresh. The camera light hard, the clean shirt clear, the pipe man clumsy, the passport left, the envelope taken, the door caught and freed.

The watcher's view.

"You have friends," square-face said, not a question.

"No," she said. "We have a room."

"Rooms do not send videos," he said.

"Ours does," she said.

The lady officer's mouth moved, not quite a smile. "Through the ashes," she read, as if tasting the title. "Is that what this is."

"It is the only way we see," she said.

Square-face looked at both of them as if measuring which set of lies had grown heavier. He nodded once, small. "Get shoes," he said. "Now."

They put shoes on. He collected his wallet, then put it back. She looked at the drawer, at the place where the note had been, at the shadow it left. She closed it again without opening.

They stepped into the corridor between two officers and two neighbours who pretended to check their locks. The watchman watched the floor.

As the door clicked shut, grey drifted out under it and into the hall like the last of something leaving.

[Watcher's Note | Day 38]

Forced entry by two male associates.
Removal attempt: partial.
Counter-presence recorded. Visual evidence transmitted.
Subsequent police arrival confirmed.
Interior materials destroyed by residents.
Status: ash residue, leverage redistribution, parties repositioned.

Downstairs, in the small wash of station light spilling from the open door, the city waited with its forms and questions and patience. He and she stood side by side on the steps, not touching, breath white in the thin night.

"Do we run," he asked.

"There is no door," she said.

They walked in.

Behind them, the apartment kept the smell of smoke and the shape of the rooms and the memory of two men who had not learned how to leave.

24

The Price of Survival

The station air was colder than outside. Tube lights hummed. A wall calendar curled at the corners. The floor smelled of phenyl and old confessions.

They put him on a metal chair in Interview Two. They put her in Interview Three. A corridor of closed doors separated them like a thin country.

He kept his palms flat on the table. He watched the way dust gathered at the edge where cloth never reached. The fan did not tick here. It buzzed.

Square-face took the seat opposite. The file lay open. He kept one finger across the spine as if the paper might try to run.

"You sleep," the officer asked.

"No."

"Good," the officer said. "People tell the truth when tired."

He waited.

"You invited men to your home," the officer said.

"They came."

"They came because doors were soft."

He said nothing.

The officer slid a printout across. Grainy still. The service lift door half open. A small figure in a corner, hand on the rail, scar like a comma on the knuckle. His.

"Groceries," the officer said, neutral.

He looked at the picture, then at the officer's face. "Yes."

"You are bleeding money," the officer said. "You try to stop it with visitors. You make mistakes. You are not clever."

He took that in.

The officer turned a page. Another still. The clean shirt lifting a drawer. The passport left. The note gone. The camera light white and flattening.

"You have friends who like to watch," the officer said. "They send us gifts. You should choose better friends."

He kept his eyes on the table. "I did not call him."

"No," the officer said. "She did."

He looked up. The room blurred for a second and then hardened again.

The officer let the silence grow. Then leaned in, elbows on the table, voice almost kind. "We can charge both of you today," he said. "Obstruction. Destruction of what may be evidence. Association. Many words. Or we can hold our breath if you give us a name that means something."

"A name for what."

"For the balcony," the officer said. "A hand on a back. A fight gone wrong. An older story under a newer one."

He swallowed. "I was not there."

"I know," the officer said, evenly. "We have you at home at the time. You are not my push. You are my pay. I am still missing the push."

He looked at the wall clock. It had no second hand. Time moved without proof.

"You want to live," the officer said. "You pay with something else."

He closed his eyes. He opened them. "I do not know who pushed."

The officer did not sigh. He fan-shuffled the photos instead, soft. "Who had a reason," he said.

"She worked at her office," he said. "She knew a secret there."

"Whose," the officer asked.

He gave a shape, not a name. "The man who does the reviews. The one who talks quietly. He wears a wedding ring he takes off for lunch."

The officer wrote one line. No name. A description. He waited. When no name arrived, he tapped the pen once on the line. "You will bring me the rest," he said. "Passwords. Calendars. Times she left. Times she came."

"My phone is with you."

"Then you will bring your memory," the officer said. "Tomorrow morning."

He nodded.

The officer closed the file halfway. "One more," he said. "Your visitor with clean shoes. He has a name."

He gave it. Softly. The officer wrote it without blinking, as if he had known all along and only wanted to see how it felt to hear it.

"Numbers," the officer said.

He recited. The officer matched it to a list in the file and made no sound.

"You will not leave the city," the officer said, a ritual now. "You will send me the locations where you were the week she fell."

He nodded again. The words felt heavier today.

The officer stood. "If you come with lies tomorrow," he said, "your price will be higher."

He sat alone after. He did not rub his eyes. He stared at the water stain in the ceiling that looked like a continent and thought about borders he could not cross.

Breather

In Interview Three the room was the same size but felt smaller. The lady officer with the braid had moved the chair slightly, so the distance from table to wall was a fraction tighter. Details like that hold people.

The ledger lay open. Blue ink. Straight lines.

"You are tired," the officer said.

"I am awake," she said.

"Good," the officer said. "People lie better when wide awake."

"Then ask me when I am almost asleep," she said.

The officer's mouth shifted, not a smile. "We have your cigarette on the balcony," she said. "We have you lying about the dead woman. We have you opening doors you should close. We do not yet have why."

She lit nothing. She clasped her hands and kept them still. "Fear," she said.

"Of what."

"Living with myself," she said.

"You knew her," the officer said.

"Yes."

"How."

She told it clean. Names held back, shapes precise. The woman at work who liked pressure. The man who gave appraisals and removed his ring at lunch. The threat. The promise. The last day.

"She leaned," the officer said.

"She smiled," she said.

"You think someone pushed."

"Yes."

"Because you want that," the officer said. "Because falling means no one owes anyone anything. Pushing means a debt."

She held the officer's eyes. "I know a push when I feel one," she said.

"Who," the officer asked.

She did not look away. "The man with the ring removed," she said. "Or the one who pays his own men to make doors soft. Both can do it. Only one would enjoy it."

The officer wrote. Not a name. A ring. A habit. Then: "You will bring me a proof I can show a judge," she said. "Chats. Emails. Calendar entries. I do not need the picture in your head."

"My phone is in your drawer," she said.

"You have a laptop at work," the officer said. "You have access. You have a memory."

She nodded. She thought of the slip of paper in the toothbrush mug at home. She thought of the watcher. She thought of the envelope gone from the drawer and the line it had left behind, like a place a picture had lived on a wall for years.

"You want to live," the officer said. "Pick a truth you can carry."

She let that sit. Then she said, "If I give you him, do you let him go."

"Him who sits here," the officer asked.

"Yes," she said.

"We do not trade like that," the officer said. "We only count."

She exhaled without smoke. She nodded again, once. "Then I will bring you both truths," she said.

"Good," the officer said, voice flat. "Tomorrow at ten."

The officer closed the ledger. The line of blue ink stopped neatly at the margin. She stood a second longer, as if something needed to be left in the room. She left nothing except the shape of her silence.

They put them on two benches after, the painted line between. He stared at the notice board. She watched the stairs. People moved. Files moved. A boy ran with a stapler.

He said without looking at her, "He wanted a name."

She said without looking at him, "So did she."

"You gave one," he said.

"I gave a direction," she said.

"Me too," he said.

They were quiet. A woman on the far bench sobbed into a towel. A constable poured water from a steel jug and spilled some and said sorry three times.

He turned his head. "I gave the number."

"His."

"Yes."

"You just bought trouble," she said.

"You bought it last night," he said.

They fell silent again. It held.

Square-face appeared. "Sign," he said, placing two statements on a clipboard.

He took the pen and read the lines slowly. She took hers and read faster. The paper did not shout. It only recorded.

He signed his name as if it were new each time. She kept her letters small, careful, as if large ones would be used against her.

Square-face took the sheets. "Tomorrow," he said. "Do not be late."

Outside the station the air felt warmer. Traffic pressed the curb. A paan stain on the wall had been washed, leaving a lighter mark shaped like a bird.

They stood near the gate, two people who had learned how not to stand close. The sun had slid behind a building and left the sky tired.

"What did you give," he asked.

"The truth that keeps us breathing," she said.

"Which one is that."

"The one where a married man prefers not to lose his job," she said. "And the one where a lender prefers not to see his face online."

"You are using both," he said.

"They used us," she said.

He looked at the road. Bikes moved around cars like fish around slow animals. "Tomorrow," he said.

"Ten," she said.

They walked home.

The watchman looked up from his stool and then looked away. A note had been taped on their door. He peeled it off and read it out loud.

Association members meeting. Agenda: safety, nuisance, eviction rules.

"Seven p.m.," she said.

He folded the note and slid it into his pocket. "They want to watch us vote ourselves out."

"We are not leaving," she said.

"We cannot," he said.

They entered. The flat smelled less of smoke now, more of wet cloth. He opened the window an inch. She closed it.

They sat without tea. They sat without cigarettes. They listened to the building.

The landline rang once. Stopped. Rang again.

He stared at it. She answered.

"You are alive," the voice said.

"For now," she said.

"Tomorrow," the voice said.

"At ten," she said.

"Bring him a name," the voice said. "Or I will bring you mine."

The line clicked.

She put the receiver down as if it were warm. He watched her hand.

"Price," he said.

"Yes," she said.

They watched the window stop moving. They watched the curtain settle.

[Watcher's Note | Day 39]

Station interviews conducted. Subjects offered transactional cooperation.
Subject M provided debt-associate identification and contact.
Subject F disclosed victim's workplace link and supervisory relationship.
Both agreed to provide digital corroboration.
Pair dynamic: aligned outward, fragile inward.
Price signals accepted.

Night stretched. The building made its small sounds. A child cried once and then dreamed. Someone boiled milk and let it climb and caught it before it fell.

He stood and opened the drawer and closed it without touching anything inside. She took the toothbrush mug and placed it behind a tin in the cabinet as if that changed geography.

"Tomorrow we choose," he said.

"We already did," she said.

"Which."

"The truth we can live with," she said.

"And the one we can't," he said.

"Yes," she said.

They went to bed without turning off the small lamp. They lay side by side, not touching, with the ceiling above them and the city around them and the watcher somewhere between.

He said into the half-dark, "If the price is me."

She said into the same air, "If the price is me."

They did not finish either sentence. The room finished both.

25

Through the Ashes of Truth

The meeting notice still sat folded on the table. *Association members. Safety, nuisance, eviction rules.*

Neither of them touched it. Neither needed to. The building had already decided.

She sat on the sofa, her hair tied back, a cigarette unlit between her fingers. He stood by the window, curtain barely open, watching the corridor light flicker. The flat had learned how to hold silence.

"They will want proof," she said.

He kept his eyes on the window. "Police or neighbours."

"Both."

At seven, the corridor filled with voices. Chairs scraped. Someone tapped a mic that squealed. The association had borrowed the community hall on the ground floor. From above, the sound reached them like the echo of a sermon.

He leaned against the wall, listening to the hum. "They're talking about us."

"They were always talking about us," she said.

"They'll vote."

"They'll vote guilty," she said.

The landline rang. He picked it up.

The voice was calm. "Tomorrow, ten. Bring me a name."

"I already gave one," he said.

"You gave a shape. I want letters."

He looked at her. She watched, cigarette still unlit.

"And if I don't."

"Then I choose for you," the voice said. "And I don't choose kindly."

Click.

He replaced the receiver. "Watcher," he said.

She lit the cigarette finally. Smoke curled like handwriting. "He's losing patience."

"So are we," he said.

At nine, the power cut. The corridor filled with the shuffle of neighbours carrying candles. From the window they saw shadows gathering, heads turning toward their door.

"They're coming up," he said.

"No," she said. "They're circling. Circles always close."

The knock came at nine-thirty. Not police. Not the watcher. Flat, hurried, neighbour-knock.

"Meeting vote," a voice called. "You sign or you leave."

He stayed frozen. She walked to the door, opened it just enough to see their faces, five of them, residents with eyes too curious to be neutral.

"We are discussing your eviction," the tallest one said.

She blew smoke through the crack. "Then discuss louder. We can't hear."

The faces tightened. One woman raised her phone, recording.

"You smoke in there," she said.

"You breathe out here," she replied, and shut the door.

They sat in the dim room, the noise downstairs swelling. His hands shook against his knees. "We're finished."

She exhaled. "Not yet. Finished comes later."

He went to the drawer, opened it, pulled out the passport. "We could run."

"Where."

"Anywhere. Train station. Bus. A city where no one knows...."

"Phones know," she said. "Faces know. Watchers know."

He gripped the passport tighter. "Better than here."

She leaned forward, scar catching the candlelight. "Better is an illusion. Survival is ugly. You still want it?"

"Yes."

"Then we give them what they want."

"Which them," he asked.

"All of them," she said.

That night, they sat at the table with a single candle between them. The flat hummed with electricity trying to come back but failing.

She pushed a slip of paper across. "His name," she said.

He read it. The married man from her office. The one who removed his ring at lunch. She had written it neat, deliberate.

He folded it. "This kills him."

She met his eyes. "It saves us."

"You don't care if he's guilty."

"I care if we live," she said.

He stood, paced, returned. He opened the drawer, took the envelope where his debts were scribbled. He pulled out another name. The clean shirt. He set it on the table.

"This kills him," he said.

She leaned back, smoke hanging. "So give both."

"They'll know we're bargaining."

"They already know," she said. "That's why they called it price."

They sat in silence. The candle guttered. Their shadows leaned across the wall, separate, then crossed, then pulled apart again.

[Watcher's Note | Day 40]

Subject F produced written identifier: victim's supervisor, married male, ring habit noted.

Subject M produced written identifier: debt associate, codename "clean shirt."
Discussion framed in survival terms, not justice.
Notable: willingness to sacrifice external parties to maintain internal unit.
Escalation imminent.

At midnight, the power returned. Lights flared. The fan ticked.

They both squinted against the sudden brightness. She stubbed out the cigarette, rubbed her eyes. He placed the folded slips back in the drawer.

"Tomorrow we live," she said.

"Tomorrow we die slower," he said.

Neither argued further.

They went to bed without touching. Between them, the lamp glowed weak and patient. The city outside roared on, horns, dogs, drunken laughter as if to remind them that even in captivity, life went on.

She whispered, "If it must be him."

He whispered back, "If it must be her."

Both lay awake, rehearsing survival in the language of betrayal.

26

Faces of Betrayal

Morning arrived like a verdict. Not loud. Final.

He boiled water and forgot the tea leaves. She watched the kettle steam and let it scream a little before turning the knob. The flat smelled of wet metal and last night's smoke.

"Ten," she said.

"Ten," he said.

They did not talk about names. The slips slept in the drawer. The drawer knew how to keep a straight face.

He went to shave. The mirror gave him a tired man with a bruise along the forearm like a river on a map. He touched it lightly. It felt like someone else's pain.

She stood by the window and counted cars. Three yellow cabs. One truck. A scooter with two schoolbags. She counted again. It kept her hands from doing something they could not undo.

When he came out, she had made tea. Two cups. Too strong. He drank it without sugar. They sat opposite each other with the drawer between.

"You ready," he asked.

"Yes," she said.

They did not move.

He reached for his wallet. She watched his hand. He watched her eyes. He stood, tucked the wallet into his back pocket, then took it out and placed it on the table again.

She smiled a little. "Honest," she said.

"Honest is a costume," he said.

"Wear it," she said.

He put the wallet back in his pocket. She took her bag and slung it over one shoulder.

"I need to take the trash," she said, light.

"I will," he said.

"You always say that," she said, already lifting the small black bag.

He watched her cross to the door. Watched her turn the bolt, slow, as if the door might object. Watched her leave with soft steps, a woman taking out what must leave.

He waited until the steps faded. Then he opened the drawer.

The two slips lay where they had slept. One with the married man's name. One with the clean shirt's. He touched neither. He opened the next slot and found her office lanyard under a folded scarf. He hesitated. Then he took it and slid it into his pocket behind the wallet. The plastic was warm from her things.

He shut the drawer.

The stairwell was cool. She stood two floors down where the light never reached and the paint peeled in quiet curls. She placed the trash bag beside a broken bucket and waited. The building made small sounds. A radio somewhere. A child's rhyme. The lift doors opening and closing without anyone stepping out.

"You have something," a voice said, even.

He stepped out of the service corner as if he had been there all along. Camera strap. Ordinary shirt. The smell of turmeric from someone's kitchen moved across his shoulder and did not touch him.

She did not greet him. She took the folded slip from her pocket and held it between two fingers. "He asked for letters," she said.

"I know," the watcher said.

"You always know," she said.

"Too late," he said. "Usually."

"Today on time," she said, and placed the slip in his palm.

He did not look at it. He put it away without breaking eye contact.

"You want a receipt," he asked.

"No," she said.

"You want a promise," he asked.

"No," she said again.

He nodded. "Then why."

"Because he wants to live," she said. "And I want him to. But not at my price "

"You think this lowers it," he asked.

"It pays part of it," she said.

He waited.

"This morning," she said, "you will send them the stills from the balcony and the stairwell again. With the ring detail. With the times. You will copy me nowhere."

"You do not like paper trails," he said.

"I am full of them," she said. "I prefer yours."

"You trade one man for another," he said.

"I trade a man for air," she said.

He slipped something back to her. Not the slip she had given. Another paper, smaller. A still photo, printed cheap. Him at the service lift rail, hand clear, knuckle scar like a comma.

"I already gave them that," she said.

193

"This one is for you," he said. "In case you forget who you are saving."

She did not look down. She slid it into her bag and felt its thin edge cut the lining.

"Ten," he said.

"Ten," she said.

She lifted the trash. He melted back into the corner. She climbed one flight with an empty bag and full hands.

He stood at the window with the curtain open a finger's width and watched nothing move. The fan ticked. He touched his pocket and felt plastic.

When she came in, he turned toward the sink and washed a clean cup. She placed the empty trash bag in the bin the way a person fits a sheet to a mattress. Tight. Perfect. As if order could keep out consequence.

"You took time," he said.

"The lift stopped," she said.

He looked at her face for the lie. It was not there. That did not mean it was not true.

They put on shoes. He checked the door twice. She watched and said nothing. They stepped into the corridor like swimmers into cold water.

The watchman did not look up. He had learned how not to.

On the ground floor the association hall door was open. The whiteboard still said Agenda. Someone had underlined safety twice. Someone had drawn a small boat beside the word eviction and shaded it in.

Outside, the road swelled with 9 a.m. A bus coughed. A boy ran with a tiffin in a plastic bag and the handle broke and the steel careered into a puddle. He laughed anyway. The city does not always understand mood.

They walked in silence to the station. They had learned the route by heart. Left at the paan shop. Right at the clinic with the faded poster of a smiling tooth. Straight past the school gate with the broken bell.

At the gate he touched his pocket again. The lanyard sat like a secret that did not change shape.

"Stop doing that," she said.

"Doing what," he said.

"Counting what you have," she said.

He put his hand by his side.

Inside, a constable nodded them through. The interview rooms waited with their clean tables and dusty corners. Square-face did not make them wait long.

"Together," he said, for once.

They sat on one side, him and her, like two people preparing for a portrait. The officer placed two files and one phone on the table. The phone was not theirs. It was the station's.

"Name," the officer said, without preface.

She answered. Letters, not shape. The married man with the ring removed at lunch. She spelled it once. The officer did not ask for it again.

The officer looked at him. "Name," he said.

He answered. The clean shirt. Not a nickname. A business card name. He spelled it. The officer's eyebrow moved a fraction that could have been approval and could have been nothing.

"Proof," the officer said.

She opened her bag and placed nothing on the table. "You have it," she said.

He tilted his head.

"The stills you asked for," she said. "The balcony with the ring. The stairwell with his hand. The login logs from the office server. The calendar entries for late meetings that were not meetings."

"You brought a laptop," he said.

"No," she said. "You brought a watcher."

Square-face did not blink. He touched the screen of the station phone once and read something only he could see. He touched it again and slid the device away. "Good morning," he said to no one and everyone.

He turned to the man. "Proof," he said again.

He cleared his throat. "He comes when doors are soft. He leaves with what he did not earn. He frightens. He will frighten more when he is embarrassed." He took a breath. "Accounts. These numbers. These transfers. I wrote them yesterday."

"You wrote them, and you kept them," the officer said.

"I kept them, and I brought them," he said.

Square-face wrote without hurry. "At noon," he said, "we will look for both men. If we find others instead, your price multiplies."

He closed the first file and opened the second. "Now the balcony," he said. "Again."

He told his version. The scream. The silence. The body. The stain that would not leave.

She told hers. The threat. The ring. The laugh. The fall that did not feel like a fall.

Square-face listened and did not say which song he liked. He asked for times. He asked for rooms. He asked for who touched whose hand last.

He laid the two signed statements from yesterday beside today's notes. The pages made a new stack. He set his finger on the top and pressed as if keeping a bird from flying.

"Ten more minutes," he said. "Then you will go."

They waited in the hum. The lady officer came in with her braid and a whisper to his ear. He nodded. He turned his head to them.

"Someone called from your landline at eight oh five," he said. "To a number that lives in your office."

"I called," she said, steady.

"Who," the officer asked.

"The receptionist," she said.

"Why," he asked.

"To ask them to keep a seat for my ghost," she said.

He did not smile. "And you," he said to the man. "Someone used a card at your building at six fifty-one. Not your card."

He froze. "Lift," he said. "I went for air."

"Your camera friend sent me a still," the officer said mildly. "You did not leave then."

Silence held the room by the throat for a slow count of five.

She turned her head an inch. "What card," she asked.

He kept his face very still. "Trash," he said.

Square-face let the lie sit where it was. He stood. "Go," he said. "Bring me more. Noon makes men honest."

They walked out into the corridor and did not look at each other. A boy ran past with a file too big for his arm and the papers fell and he laughed and picked them up and put them back in any order and kept running.

Outside the gate the sun had moved an inch. The day had not.

Breather

They chose the long way home. Not for scenery. For breath. She walked a step ahead. He watched the back of her neck and the way the hair there always escaped. He wanted to reach and tuck it back. He did not.

At the paan shop he stopped. "Water," he said.

She waited in the shade of the tree where the bark peeled like a map. He stood at the steel drum and drank from a plastic glass rinsed twice. The water tasted of iron and someone else's story.

When he turned, she was on the phone. Not the landline. The watchman's mobile in her hand. She spoke low and fast. He caught two words. Calendar. Exports. She thanked the watchman and gave the phone back and they walked.

"Who," he asked.

"Reception," she said.

"You said it already," he said.

"I am saying it again," she said. "Because sometimes saying a thing twice is the only way to make it true."

They reached the gate. The watchman kept his eyes on his register as if the paper could save him.

Upstairs, the flat waited with its furniture at attention. The drawer closed. The tea cups dry. The single curtain pushed to one side like a picture taken off a wall that still held its shadow.

She put her bag on the chair and went to the sink and turned the tap and turned it off. He stood by the table and opened the drawer and closed it again without touching anything.

"Where is my card," she asked, casual as a question about weather.

He did not flinch. "In your bag."

She looked. She made her face into a calm room. "It is not," she said.

"Then you left it," he said.

"I do not leave things," she said.

They stood with that line between them.

The landline rang. Both looked. Neither moved. It rang out. It rang again. She picked it up.

"You sent it," the voice said.

"Yes," she said.

"Good," the voice said.

"Did he send it," she asked.

"Yes," the voice said. "He sent something else too."

"What," she asked.

"A card used at dawn," the voice said. "An empty corridor. A hand on a lanyard. We like hands in our pictures."

She closed her eyes. "Thank you," she said, and put the receiver down like it was heavier than it looked.

He watched her. "Well," he said.

"Well," she said.

He took the lanyard from his pocket and placed it on the table. No flourish. No apology. He let the plastic make its small sound against the wood.

"You went," she said.

"No," he said. "I did not leave the building."

"You planned to," she said.

"Yes," he said. "If you failed."

Her mouth tightened. "You do not give me a chance to fail," she said.

"You do not give me a chance to live," he said.

201

They breathed together for a minute that did not feel like time.

"Why her," she asked. "Why the photo. Why keep it."

"Because she was a person who did not disappear when my eyes were closed," he said. "Because once someone smiles and it is uncomplicated, you think you should keep a copy."

"She complicated us," she said.

He nodded. "I know."

"Then throw it," she said.

"It is gone," he said.

She believed him and did not.

Breather

They ate silence for lunch. Rice that stuck. A pickle that bit hard and said nothing.

At one thirty he stood. "I will go," he said.

"For what," she asked.

"To return a thing that is not mine," he said, and slipped the lanyard back into her bag.

"You keep nothing well," she said.

"You take nothing lightly," he said.

They met each other's eyes and looked away.

At two the station phone pinged. Not theirs. Far away. The watcher's packet landed where Square-face liked his gifts to land. Stills. Times. Names. A calendar entry titled Review and a location that was not the office. A booking at a bar by the sea. Two glasses. A check signed in a careful, guilty hand. The ring in the pocket. The ring on again the next day.

At three the other search landed. Accounts that were not accounts. Loans that were not loans. A ledger in a back room. A photograph of polished shoes with the pipe man laughing behind him and a wall calendar that put both at the building on the wrong morning.

At four the station desk called their landline. "Tomorrow," the lady officer said. "Early."

They said yes.

[Watcher's Note | Day 41]

Morning: Subject F delivered identifier to third-party channel. Subject M removed Subject F office card, intent inferred, returned same under pressure.
Station: both provided names. Visual corroborations received from independent source.
Afternoon: additional financial records received.
Net effect: mutual survival efforts continue, internal trust degraded but intact.

Evening came slow. The association announced a second meeting. The whiteboard now said Resolution. Someone had drawn scales and colored one side black.

She stood at the window and did not smoke. He sat at the table and did not open the drawer.

"Tomorrow," he said.

"Tomorrow," she said.

"What do we bring," he asked.

"Everything we can live with," she said.

"And what we cannot," he asked.

"We let the watcher deliver," she said.

He nodded. It felt like signing a paper without reading it.

They left the lights on and the fan turning. The room looked almost clean. A place where two people could live. If life were only furniture.

Night slid in with the sound of a scooter on the lane and two boys laughing about a match. She lit a cigarette and did not draw. He took it from her fingers and put it out.

"We will not burn today," he said.

"Tomorrow then," she said.

They lay down without sheets. The city hummed. Somewhere a pressure cooker hissed, and someone tapped the lid with a spoon to say enough.

He said into the dark, "I am sorry I took it."

She said into the same dark, "I am not sorry I gave it."

He turned his face to the wall.

She turned her face to the window.

The drawer sat between them like a third person who knew both better than they knew themselves.

27

The Last Night Together

The flat had gone quiet again. Too quiet, as if it was holding breath with them.

She closed the curtains, thick enough to block the corridor light. He switched off the fan though the air was heavy. The silence swelled with every small sound: the clink of her lighter, the faint scrape of his chair, the sigh of fabric against skin.

"Tomorrow," she said.

"Tomorrow," he said.

It had become a word neither of them trusted.

They ate late. Rice, thin dal, nothing left to dress it. Neither complained. Halfway through, she pushed her plate away. He scraped his clean until the steel showed.

When the dishes were done, when the ashtray was cleared, when there was nothing else left to occupy their hands, they sat opposite each other at the table.

"You're tired," he said.

"I'm waiting," she said.

"For what."

"For us to stop pretending this is survival."

He leaned back, looked at the ceiling. "What is it then."

"Slow murder," she said.

The landline rang once. They didn't answer. It rang again. They let it. When it stopped, the silence afterward felt deeper than before.

He rose first, restless. Crossed to the drawer. Opened it. Closed it again. His movements were mechanical, not choices but rituals. She watched him without blinking.

"Do you regret," she asked finally.

"Regret what."

"Not me. The life before me."

He thought, scratched the bruise on his arm, let the sting remind him he was still present. "I regret owing," he said.

She nodded. "I regret owing too."

"To whom."

"Myself," she said.

It was near midnight when the city began to settle, horns fading, dogs shifting to alleys, vendors pulling carts into dark corners. In the flat, neither had moved.

Then she stood. Walked to the window. Looked out at the narrow strip of road. "They're still watching," she said.

"Always," he said.

"Then let them watch this," she said, and turned.

They came together not like lovers but like survivors who had run out of barricades. The first kiss was dry, almost formal, as if signing a contract neither wanted but both understood. Then it broke, and the second was hungrier, pulling at the quiet, at the lies, at the weight of everything unsaid.

Her shirt came off first. Not tossed, not hurried, just peeled away like a scab she'd stopped pretending to need. He undressed slower, as though he feared the act itself was a confession.

There was no seduction in it. Only inevitability. Their bodies knew what was expected and went through the steps. The touch of skin on skin was both balm and wound.

On the bed, they moved without rhythm, without grace. His hand on her scar. Her fingers pressing the bruise on his arm. Both seeking proof of existence, not comfort.

At one point she stopped, looked at him hard. "Did you push her."

His breath caught. "No."

"Did you want to."

He swallowed. "Yes."

Her eyes didn't flinch. "Then we're even."

She rolled on top of him, took what she needed, left nothing gentle behind.

After, they lay back, chests rising and falling in uneven time. Sweat cooled on their skin. The sheet tangled between them like a third body.

He said into the dark, "If they ask me tomorrow, I'll say your name."

She exhaled smoke toward the ceiling. "If they ask me, I'll say yours."

They both smiled, faint, bitter.

"Maybe that's the only way we survive," he said.

"Maybe that's the only way we die together," she said.

[Watcher's Note | Day 42]

Subjects engaged in physical intimacy, high tension context.
Verbal exchange: mutual accusation, mutual survival pact framed as betrayal.
Notable: both acknowledged willingness to sacrifice the other at formal inquiry.
Assessment: final convergence before fracture.

Toward dawn, she woke first. Sat by the window, naked under the sheet, cigarette glowing faint red. The city was beginning to stir, milk vans, paper boys, restless horns. She blew smoke against the glass, left no mark.

He stirred, sat up, rubbed his face. Watched her back, the outline of her shoulders, the curve of the sheet.

"You're leaving," he said.

"Not yet," she said.

"When."

"When there's no other choice."

He nodded, though she couldn't see.

She came back to the bed. Curled into him, her head on his chest. He stroked her hair once, then stopped.

"If this is the last night," he said.

"It is," she said, eyes closed.

"Then remember me...."

"As what," she cut in.

He searched. "As someone who stayed."

She smiled faintly against his skin. "No one stays. Not really."

The fan ticked. Outside, a crow cawed once, harsh and early. They lay in silence until sleep claimed them both, light, fragile, temporary.

When morning came, they rose without touching. They dressed in silence. She tied her hair. He buttoned his shirt wrong, then fixed it.

The slips of paper in the drawer waited. So did the city. So did the watcher.

They stepped out together, side by side, knowing the last night they would ever truly share was behind them.

28

The Twist

They called them in before nine.

The station smelled like wet paperwork. Square-face stood beside a desk monitor. The lady officer with the braid had a pen in her hair and tired eyes that still saw everything.

"Stand here," Square-face said.

They stood. Close but not touching.

The monitor woke. Grainy black and white. A timestamp in the corner. A corridor with a cheap runner rug. Opposite building. Third floor.

The door opened in the frame. A man stepped out first. Shirt sleeves rolled. Hair neat in a way that took time. He looked both ways and wiped his mouth with the back of his hand like a teenager caught after a kiss.

Her boss.

She exhaled once, slow.

Ananya stepped out after him. Hair open. Cigarette in two fingers. She leaned against the wall and smiled at him. The cigarette stayed unlit. She liked to hold things that burned without using them.

The officer tapped the keyboard. Another angle. A small dome camera at the stair landing. The same corridor from above. You could see the door, the cheap rug, the corner of the balcony rail at the end.

Ananya lifted the cigarette to her lips and spoke without looking at the man. He took her hand and then dropped it when he remembered cameras exist. He patted his pockets for a lighter and found nothing. She laughed.

A third figure entered the frame.

A woman. Saree draped practical. Hair tied tight. Face still. She did not run. She walked like someone who already knew the floor plan.

The wife.

Ananya saw her first. The smile hardened. The man took one step back, mouth opening, then closing, body already building a story he could live with later.

The wife did not look at him. She looked at Ananya.

"Listen," he said. The audio was dead. Only mouths moved. Only hands said things.

The wife moved closer. Not fast. Not violent yet. She spoke. Ananya answered. No one looked at the camera. The lens watched without blinking.

The wife lifted a hand. Not to slap. To point. Ananya laughed once and did not move aside. The man made a small shape with his hands like a peace sign without the peace. He put his palm on the wife's arm. She shook him off without using any more strength than necessary.

The wife took the unlit cigarette out of Ananya's hand and snapped it in half. It looked like a magic trick. Ash puffed. Ananya's mouth tightened. She stepped to the rail. Not escape. Stance.

They stood like that. Three bodies at angles. For a moment it looked like a sculpture made of bad choices.

Then motion. Not clear. Not wild. Just a pivot. A hand reached. Which hand. The camera did not care. The wife's shoulder moved forward. Ananya stepped back without meaning to. The man flinched toward them and then away as if pulled by two magnets.

The frame shivered once. The world dropped one breath.

Ananya hit the rail with her hip. She reached for it. Fingers closed around iron. The wife moved again, small, precise. The hand that had snapped a cigarette found a wrist and peeled it off metal. The man's mouth opened in a shape that would later become the word jump.

Ananya went over.

No sound. Only exit. The camera held the corridor while the end of the frame forgot what it had held.

Silence in the room. The monitor showed the man frozen in place and the wife with her palm flat on the rail as if measuring it. Both looked down at the absence.

Square-face paused the footage. The timestamp blinked.

He spoke without turning. "There is more," he said "The lift."

Another window opened. The old elevator camera. Earlier that night. The wife inside, face lifted to the numbers, hand tucked under her saree pleats. She held a phone to her ear. The screen showed the number dialled. The lady officer read it out loud.

She gave a name.

They both knew it.

Her.

Her number. The one she had given at the bar without thinking. The one that lived on business cards and delivery receipts and office rosters.

She did not flinch. "Open the audio," she said.

"There is none," Square-face said. "But there is a record."

The ledger appeared. Call logs. Outgoing from wife's phone to hers. A minute and nine seconds. Nine minutes before the corridor.

He shifted, looked at her. She did not look away.

The screen changed again. A screenshot from a chat box. The wife's number. A message posted earlier that evening from an unlisted account. A link. A line.

He is there now. Third floor. Door with red paint. Don't bring the ring.

Square-face looked up. "The account was created same day. The IP traces to a coffee shop you like. Camera shows you at that table. You were in frame nineteen minutes."

She inhaled.

The officer did not gather herself into triumph. She only blinked slower. "You did not push," she said. "You placed."

The room held the word.

He spoke, voice rough. "You set her up."

She turned her head toward him. "I told a wife the time."

"You led her to murder."

"I led her to truth," she said.

"Truth with a rail," he said.

Square-face let them say it. He closed the chat window and opened a fourth. A lobby camera from later. The man and the wife leaving separately. The man wiping his eyes with a handkerchief he did not use for tears. The wife rolling her ring around her finger once and sliding it back home.

The officer turned the monitor off. The dark screen reflected them all. The three in the room. The two at the table. One in a chair ten years older than all of them.

"Tell me," Square-face said, gentle as a doctor before pain. "Why him."

She kept her voice even. "Because he took what he wanted and called it review."

"And why her," he asked.

"Because she wanted to be seen and I am tired of being the only one who is," she said.

He looked at her. "You understand that you built a fall."

She nodded. "I did not plan the push."

"You planned the meeting," he said. "The rest is a small walk."

He turned to the man. "You did not push. You paid. You invited violence when you needed it to visit your house for a different reason. You cannot carry the balcony, but you carry the pipe."

He swallowed. "I did not want anyone to die."

"Everyone says that," Square-face said.

The lady officer's pen stopped moving. "We will call her," she said. "The wife. We will call him. The husband. They will sit where you sit. They will think we do not know and then learn that we do."

A knock on the door. A constable slipped in with a note folded twice. Square-face read it. He kept his face flat.

"Your watcher sent a present," he said.

He laid a small envelope on the table and tipped it. A flash drive slid out. No label. The plastic dull.

"Another angle," the officer said.

They watched because their eyes had learned not to stop.

Same corridor. Same night. Not the building's camera. A different grain. Cleaner. Something like a phone propped against a wall decor. The frame caught more of the rail.

They saw exactly what the corridor camera did not want to see. The wife taking the wrist. Ananya's fingers slipping. The tiny gap between iron and skin widening. The man raising a hand and not using it. His hand hanging in air like a guilty flag. The wife's mouth forming a word whose shape looked like enough.

Then air where a body used to be.

218

The wife's face, when she looked up, was not monstrous. It was tired. It was a woman seeing a life she built tilt.

The clip ended there. The room air turned heavy.

"Your watcher had this," the officer said. "But not for us. Not at first."

Square-face took the drive between two fingers and held it like something that bit. "He tells me it was a job before it was a hobby. The wife hired him months ago. He watched the husband. Then he watched everyone. Then he watched himself."

He turned the drive in his hand. "He serves himself," Square-face said quietly. "But even that brings something to me."

She closed her eyes for a breath. When she opened them, the world was the same. "You will arrest them," she said.

"We will invite them," the officer said. "We do not embarrass houses if we can avoid it. We only shake them until the crockery speaks."

He looked at her. "And you."

She waited.

"You will sit with us tomorrow again," he said. "You will bring your messages. You will bring the account you made. You will bring the coffee shop bill. You will sign something that uses the word instigation without saying it."

He looked at him. "And you. You will bring your friend in the clean shirt, or I will fetch him with shoes that do not smile."

They did not ask to go. The officer told them. "Go," she said. "Do not leave the city. That line grows old in my mouth."

They stepped into the corridor where a boy ran past with a stamp pad and left a finger mark on the wall for no reason at all.

Outside the station the light felt loud. They stood on the pavement with scooters brushing their hips and vendors shouting about oranges and one stray dog sleeping with its head on its paws.

He said, "You called her."

"Yes."

"You wanted this."

"I wanted witness," she said.

"You chose the wife," he said.

"She was always in the room," she said. "She just had the lights off."

He looked at the road. "You killed her."

"I did not touch her," she said.

"Your hand was the first push," he said.

She did not argue. She lit a cigarette and let the smoke climb.

They walked back in a line that was not together. At the gate the watchman kept his eyes down. They took the stairs because the lift seemed like a small confession.

In the flat the air felt thinner than morning. The drawer sat where it always sat. The passport kept its secrets. The ashtray waited.

He pulled a chair out and sat. He did not take off his shoes.

She stood by the window and looked at the opposite balcony. The stain was still faint. The angle of the rail had not learned regret.

"She did not scream on the way down," she said.

"How do you know," he asked.

"I was at my window," she said. "The glass remembered."

He lifted his head. "You watched."

"I watch everything now," she said.

The landline rang. He answered this time.

A quiet voice. Calm. "We finished a job," it said.

"The wife," he asked.

"The truth," the voice said.

He waited.

"I had the angle," the voice said. "I did not hand it because it was not ready. Today it was."

"You work for her," he said.

"I work for whatever pays for the next angle," the watcher said. "Today the angle paid me."

"What now," he asked.

"Now the city does its slow work," the watcher said. "You bring paper. They bring mouth. I bring light when no one invites it."

"Why give it now," he asked.

"Because everyone thinks they are the author," the watcher said. "Sometimes they need a full stop."

The line clicked. The room got quiet again.

She turned from the window. "He will keep us alive," she said.

"He will keep us interesting," he said.

She sat. The chair creaked in a way that sounded like a tired laugh.

"Say it," he said.

"What."

"That I killed her," he said.

She looked at him. "You are not my push," she said. "You are my mirror."

He breathed out.

"Say it," she said.

"What."

"That I brought her to the rail," she said.

He looked at her a long time. "You did," he said.

She nodded.

They let the sentence sit between them. Then she stood and walked to the sink and ran water and turned it off.

"Tomorrow," he said.

"Tomorrow," she said.

They did not touch. They did not cry. They did not plan. They sat in the same room with something larger than them and watched it choose a chair.

New visual obtained from private source.
Sequence confirms physical push by spouse,
preceded by Subject F's contact and
location disclosure.
Subject M role unchanged: debt-driven
facilitation in separate event stream.
Investigation posture: spouse and
supervisor to be interviewed as primaries;
subjects retained as cooperating witnesses
pending material corroboration.
Apartment remains central witness site.

Evening made a slow turn. Across the street someone watered plants on a balcony. Water fell in a silver line and broke into nothing before it touched ground. The stain stayed.

He said, "If they ask what you wanted."

She said, "I will say I wanted a story where I did not go quiet."

"And if they ask what I wanted."

"You wanted an end that did not cost my name," she said.

The fan turned. It did not click this time. The room noticed and did not mention it.

Outside, a child clapped, delighted by a small violence that hurt no one.

They sat until the light changed and the curtain edges went from grey to dark. They did not turn on a lamp. They let the city set the dimness for them.

When it got too quiet, he spoke into the space between them. "Who really killed her."

She tilted her head. "Three people," she said. "One with a hand. Two with a need."

He thought about that. He nodded once, small.

"Who lives," he asked.

She looked at him. "People who learn to carry what they caused," she said.

He closed his eyes. "We will try."

"We already are," she said.

They sat with that. The room held it without dropping.

29

No Exit

Morning started with a thud.

A notice taped to their door. He peeled it off and read aloud because reading made things real.

Resolution: Eviction proceedings initiated. Water supply subject to restriction until compliance.

She took the paper, folded it once, slid it under the sugar tin. "They cut the wrong thing," she said. "They should cut air."

The tap coughed when he tried it. A thin brown stream, then nothing. He let it run anyway, as if persistence could coax a city to change its mind.

The bell rang before eight. Not a neighbour tap. A professional ring.

He opened.

Square-face. The lady officer with the braid. Two constables behind, bored eyes, steady feet.

"We will not take long," Square-face said.

She stepped aside. The officers entered like people who have already been here in their heads.

The lady officer stood near the sink, looked once at the dry tap, and wrote a small line on a small pad. "How much water stored," she asked.

"Enough for tea," she said.

"Make none," the officer said. "We have work."

Square-face set a folder on the table and did not open it. "We need formal statements under the magistrate," he said. "Today."

He looked from one to the other. "Before that, we need to collect certain items you promised."

She nodded at her bag. "Office login. Calendar exports. The bill from the coffee shop."

He nodded. "And yours," he said to him.

He took out the paper with numbers. The ledger copies. The names of men who liked doors soft. He placed them beside the folder and kept his hands flat so they would not tremble.

A constable moved to the landline and took a photograph of its call log printout pinned by a magnet. The lady officer opened the sugar tin and removed the folded eviction notice and returned it to the table, neat, as if organization lowered heat.

"Come," Square-face said. "We go now. You will be back before the building learns to clap."

She grabbed her bag. He patted his pocket for a wallet he did not need and put it back anyway. They locked the door out of habit. It made no difference.

The watchman did not look up when they passed him. His register had become a shield.

Outside, the day was pale and honest. They rode in separate cars.

The courthouse corridor had windows that faced a wall. Light came in sideways and stayed on the floor like a tired dog.

He sat on a wooden bench outside a small door that said Magistrate. A clerk with ink on his fingers held a tray of pens like they might escape. Square-face leaned against the opposite wall, eyes on nothing, mind on everything.

A peon called his name. He stood. The door swallowed him.

Inside, the room was smaller than he imagined. The magistrate wore no drama. His voice was light, almost bored.

"Do you understand why you are here," the magistrate asked.

"Yes."

"You are free to speak or not," the magistrate said. "If you speak, it will be written. If you sign, it will be used."

He nodded.

Square-face stood back. The stenographer lifted her chin. The air felt thinner.

"Who was in your house the night the men entered," the magistrate asked.

He answered carefully. Dates. Times. The clean shirt. The pipe. The camera that made light inside darkness. He said he did not call the watcher. He said she did.

"Who left the bolt soft," the magistrate asked.

"I did," he said, voice low.

"Why," the magistrate asked.

"I thought I could control the price," he said.

"Who pushed the woman from the balcony," the magistrate asked.

"The wife," he said.

"Who set the meeting," the magistrate asked.

He looked at the floor. The dot of old chewing gum there had trapped dust for years. "She told the wife where to find them," he said.

"Names," the magistrate asked.

He gave them. Full. Clean.

The stenographer's keys clicked like rain that did not cool a thing.

"Do you say this by force," the magistrate asked.

"No."

"Any promise," the magistrate asked.

"No."

"You read," the magistrate said. The sheet slid toward him, new ink, his words returning in a different voice. He read slowly. Nothing surprised him. Everything did.

"Sign," the magistrate said.

His hand did not shake when he wrote his name. It shook when he put the pen down.

Outside, Square-face took the document, slid it into a brown file, and did not comment. "Wait there," he said, nodding toward the bench.

He sat. He listened to a fan that squeaked every third rotation. He watched the clerk sort pens by height and then unsort them again.

She was taken to a different room down a different corridor. The lady officer sat beside her, not across. A gesture that looked like sympathy and was also strategy.

The magistrate repeated the ritual. Choice. Use. Ink.

"Why did you contact the wife," he asked.

She spoke in a voice that did not ask for forgiveness. "Because he would not stop," she said. "Because review meant touch. Because she deserved to know how her days lived when she was not in them."

"You foresaw the balcony," he asked.

"I foresaw a fight," she said.

"You foresaw the rail," he asked.

"I foresaw anger," she said.

"Who pushed," he asked.

"The wife," she said.

"And who built the stair to that moment," he asked.

She closed her eyes for a breath. "I told her where to go," she said.

"Names," he asked.

She gave them. Full. Clean.

"Who left the door soft for the men who came later," he asked.

She did not blink. "He did," she said.

"Why," he asked.

"Because he thinks people can be negotiated like bills," she said.

The sheet came. The words returned. She read. Her mouth did not move.

"Sign," he said.

Her hand did not shake.

When she stepped into the corridor, the lady officer took nothing from her face. "Water?" she asked.

"No," she said.

"Food?"

"No."

"Then go," the officer said gently. "Sit with him and pretend you still have breath to share."

They sat on the same bench, not touching. The hallway smelled of ink and old files. Time did not move.

He said quietly, "You signed."

"So did you," she said.

He looked at her hands. A black smudge of carbon under her ring finger where ink had tried to stay. He wanted to wipe it with his thumb and did not.

Square-face returned with two receipts and a next step. "Ten tomorrow," he said. "Bring your devices. If your office complains, give them my number. If your lender complains, give him my eyes."

They stood. "Can we go home," he asked.

Square-face nodded. "Home," he said. "Until your building decides it prefers someone else."

By late afternoon the corridor in their floor had new decorations. A camera bubble at the ceiling corner. A sign below it: Under watch for resident safety.

She laughed without sound. "The city learns fast," she said.

The watchman looked up as they entered the gate. He almost stood, then remembered something and remained seated.

Upstairs, a white envelope lay under their door. No seal. No handwriting.

Inside: a single photograph. Him, inside the magistrate's room, signing. Her, in a different room, signing. Two frames printed on one sheet, side by side, like a wedding card made by a person who disliked marriage.

She held it without speaking. He reached for it and stopped before his hand reached paper.

"Who sent this," he asked.

"Someone who enjoys full stops," she said.

She placed the photo on the table like a small plate and did not sit. She walked to the sink, turned the tap, watched air hiss. She returned.

They stood on either side of the photograph and stared at the proof that both needed to survive and neither could forgive.

"You told them my part," he said.

"You told them mine," she said.

The sentence hung. It did not break.

He sat finally. His chair complained. He put his palms flat on the table, the way he had at the station.

"I thought we would lie together," he said.

"We did," she said. "Until truth paid better."

He looked up. "For who."

"For both," she said. "Just not in the same currency."

The fan clicked on its fourth turn. He looked at it as if it might decode speech.

The landline rang. He let it. It rang out. Rang again. She answered.

"Water returns at six," a polite association voice said. "Toilet use only. Kindly cooperate with committee decisions."

She thanked him as if he were human.

The bell rang again. Neighbours this time, a small group, faces tight with civic duty. The tall man held a clipboard.

"Society vote passed," he said. "Vacate within seven days."

She exhaled. "We do not have seven."

"You have five legally," he said. "We gave you two extra."

He handed over a copy of the resolution. He added in a lower voice, almost kind, "Leave early. It is easier."

She took the paper and shut the door softly. "They called it safety," she said.

"It is," he said. "For everyone else."

They did not speak for a while. Evening sidled in. The corridor light clicked on. Footsteps went about the business of other lives.

He opened the drawer because that was what he did when silence grew. The passport. The slips. The photograph of the balcony long burned its ghost still in the wood.

He took out nothing. He put nothing in. He closed it.

She moved to the window and looked at the opposite rail. A woman watered plants. Water fell and evaporated before the ground remembered it.

"You can go," he said, eyes on the table. "Take your bag. Take your name. The police have enough. You will be witness. They will let you breathe in a place where neighbours do not vote you out before dinner."

"And you," she asked.

"I will not fit anywhere that is not this room," he said.

She turned. "Do not ask me to choose you over air," she said.

He stared at the photograph of their signatures. "I am not asking you anything," he said. "I am telling you the door does not open for me anymore."

"Doors open," she said. "People refuse."

He laughed once, tired. "They open to show me another wall," he said.

She came closer, stopped at the edge of the small square of lamplight that made the table look like a stage. "If I go," she said, "do you give me your name to carry as luggage."

He shook his head. "Carry only what you can lift without help," he said. "I am heavy."

The landline rang again. He picked it up this time.

"You signed well," the voice said.

He did not ask who. He knew.

"You had the angle," he said.

"I always do," the watcher said. "Now I have the ending."

"This is not ending," he said.

"For some," the watcher said. "For others it is a pause written as a period."

"Why send the photograph," he asked.

"So you do not lie to each other about the part where you did what was needed," the watcher said. "People prefer stories where they kept promises. I prefer the ones where they kept breath."

"What do you want next," he asked.

"Nothing," the watcher said. "I will watch your building committee practice democracy. I will watch police practice mercy. I will watch you practice goodbye."

The line clicked.

He put the receiver down slowly. She watched his hand.

"Watcher," she said.

"Yes."

"What did he say."

"That we are interesting when we break," he said.

She nodded as if that were mathematics.

He stood. "I will pack one bag," he said. "It will not be heavy."

She watched him open the cupboard and take shirts that did not know if they would be worn again. He put them in the small backpack he kept for laundry. He added nothing else.

She went to the bathroom and lifted her toothbrush mug. The bottom was damp with residue from water that was no longer there. The slip with his numbers was still tucked behind it. She took it out, looked at the ink that had not blurred, and slid it back.

When she came out, he was at the door with the backpack on one shoulder. He was not leaving. He was practicing.

"Where will you go," she asked.

"I will walk until the city decides where I stop," he said.

"Tonight," she asked.

"Not yet," he said. "We are not finished with the part where the walls tell us what we cost."

She set her bag by the chair and did not zip it.

They waited for six. At six the building made a sound like an old throat clearing. The tap spat and filled a plastic bucket two inches and then stopped. The water smelled faintly of iron and triumph.

"Toilet use only," she said.

He laughed without humour. "The city knows how to humiliate politely," he said.

The bell rang. Not a neighbour. Police again. Square-face alone this time. No constables. No braid.

He held up a single sheet. "Acknowledgement," he said. "You sign that you received the eviction." He set it on the table with a pen.

They signed. Square-face pocketed it.

"You have a place," he asked.

"No," she said.

"Find one by Friday," he said. "We do not like to come for furniture."

He turned to leave, then paused. "You will both come tomorrow," he said. "Bring what remains. The wife arrives at eleven. She will not lie well. The husband at one. He will."

He looked at their faces like a doctor looks at a patient who needs sleep and something stronger. "Rest," he said. "Tonight is the last quiet one."

He left.

"Quiet," he said to the room. "He does not know us."

"Quiet is a word for houses that have no memory," she said.

Night bloomed outside. The corridor calmed. The new camera bubble held a small circle of light as if cupping evening in a hand.

They sat across from each other without tea. The photograph of their signatures lay between them like a map they were both bad at reading.

"I did not plan to sign," he said.

"Neither did I," she said.

"But we did," he said.

"Yes," she said.

"We are finished," he said.

"No," she said. "We are just out of exits."

He looked at the backpack. "Will you come if I walk," he asked.

"No," she said. "I will come if you stay and tell the truth you can live with."

"Which one is that," he asked.

"The one where we both caused it," she said. "And neither of us can be forgiven for the part we gave away."

He nodded. It felt like a confession that did not need a priest.

They did not touch that night. They did not sleep. They did not plan. They sat until the photograph on the table curled at one corner in the humid air and lay flat again.

Society eviction resolution delivered.
Water restricted.
Magistrate statements recorded for both subjects.
Visual confirmation produced to residence.
Pair dynamic: fracture declared, cohabitation maintained pending relocation.
Police follow-up scheduled with spouse and supervisor.
No exit pathways observed that do not increase cost.

Dawn came slow. The city stretched. A vendor shouted about bread.

He lifted the backpack and set it down again.

She picked up the photograph and tore it clean across the middle. Her half she kept. The other she left on the table.

"Why," he asked.

"So you cannot pretend we did not choose," she said.

He nodded, and for the first time since morning he smiled, brief and hopeless and real.

"Then it is settled," he said.

"It is," she said.

They faced the door that would not let them out and waited for it to tell them what came next.

30

Courtroom or Confession

The courtroom was small, almost windowless, its walls damp with old verdicts. A ceiling fan turned, not to cool, but to remind everyone that the air moved only when told.

He sat at one table, she at another. Between them: a narrow aisle, a clerk with a stack of printouts, and a magistrate who looked like a man pulled from bed too early.

Square-face stood near the window. The lady officer with the braid hovered by the files. Neither spoke. The papers would speak now.

The clerk began to read.

"Exhibit One. A WhatsApp message, dated three weeks before incident."

The clerk's voice was flat, merciless.

Her: *'You live here alone?'*
Him: *'Yes.'*
Her: *'Good.'*

The magistrate's eyes lifted briefly. "Good?"

She did not look away. "I meant safe," she said.

The clerk continued.

"Exhibit Two. Voice note, recovered from Subject M's phone backup."

The tape hissed. His voice, low, tired.

'If they ask me tomorrow, I'll say your name.'

Her voice replied, faint, almost a whisper.

'If they ask me, I'll say yours.'

The room tightened. The magistrate leaned forward. "This is confession," he said.

"It is intimacy," she countered.

"It is pact," he added

"Pacts become evidence," Square-face said.

The clerk shuffled. "Exhibit Three. Banking app log-ins, cross-shared passwords. Mutual access."

He read without pause. Account names. Times. Transactions. Each one now a nail in a coffin neither had thought they were building.

"Interpretation," the magistrate said.

The braid officer spoke. "Two subjects lived as one unit. Access implies trust. But also complicity."

He leaned forward. "I never touched her accounts."

The braid officer raised her brow. "Your fingerprints unlocked her phone."

Her laugh cut the air, sharp. "He wanted to. He didn't need to."

"Exhibit Four. Deleted images, recovered from cloud."

The projector screen lit. Grainy pictures, the two of them on the sofa, the curve of her smile, the weight of his arm, their clothes loosened, their eyes half-closed. Intimate. Ordinary.

But the caption beneath each file was different: *Proof of proximity. Proof of concealment. Proof of intimacy beyond witness.*

He clenched his jaw. "You use our bodies like weapons."

The magistrate tapped the table. "Bodies are weapons. Sometimes they wound, sometimes they testify."

She stared at the screen, calm. "They are not lies," she said.

"No," he said. "They are worse. They are truths in the wrong hands."

The clerk cleared his throat. "Exhibit Five. Audio from landline. Call at 8:05 p.m. Recipient: office reception."

The tape hissed. Her voice again.

'He's there now. Don't bring the ring.'

The magistrate lifted his head. "You sent her to the balcony."

Her scar caught the light as she tilted her chin. "I gave her a choice."

"You gave her a map," he snapped.

"Maps don't push," she said coldly.

Square-face stepped forward. He opened the folder he had not touched until now. Inside: two sheets, their statements from the day before. He placed them side by side.

"Read," he said.

They both did. Their words, neat in black ink. His line: *She told the wife where to go.* Her line: *He left the door soft.*

The magistrate tapped both. "So you agree, each points to the other. Each agrees the other is guilty."

She said, "Each agrees the other survived."

He said, "Each agrees survival costs blood."

The braid officer stood, held up another slip. "Exhibit Six. The note slid under their door."

The magistrate read aloud: *'One of you pushed. One of you paid. Both of you lie.'*

He looked up. "Anonymous. But accurate."

The silence that followed was not empty. It was crowded, pressing against skin.

"Do you wish to amend your statements?" the magistrate asked.

She said, "No."

He said, "No."

The magistrate leaned back, weary. "Then you have confessed enough. Both are complicit. Neither innocent."

He signed a paper, quick, impatient. "Adjourned until wife and husband appear. Eleven. One."

The gavel was not struck. It did not need to be. The silence was heavier.

Outside, they were escorted down the corridor, side by side but apart. The walls seemed closer, the steps louder.

At the gate, the constables let them go. "Tomorrow," Square-face said. "Do not vanish."

They walked in the direction of home. Not together. Not separate.

Back in the flat, the air stank of damp paper and smoke. The photograph of their signatures still lay torn on the table. She touched the half she had kept. He dropped his keys into the chipped bowl.

"You told them my part," he said.

"You told them mine," she said.

"It was not lie," he said

"Nor mine," she said.

They looked at each other, not with love, not with hate, but with the clarity of two people who had signed their own ending.

[Watcher's Note | Day 45]

Subject M statement: confirms Subject F directed spouse.
Subject F statement: confirms Subject M facilitated debt intrusion.
Both maintain survival through mutual betrayal.
Court exhibits include: chats, calls, images, passwords.
Assessment: intimacy has become confession.
Prosecution leverage increased.

That night, they did not cook. They did not speak. They sat in the same room with the hum of the city outside.

Finally, she said, "Do you still want me to stay."

He closed his eyes. "I want no one. I want no exits. I want sleep without rails."

She lit a cigarette and smoked in silence.

The flat listened. The flat remembered. The flat waited for tomorrow, when others would enter and speak louder truths.

31

The Last Night Together (Again)

The city slept like a liar, restless under its own noise, pretending at calm.
Their flat did not sleep at all.

The day had stripped them bare. Court exhibits, signatures, WhatsApp threads dressed up as weapons. Now only the night remained, and in that night, there was no shield left between them.

He sat at the table with the torn photograph. She leaned by the window, cigarette balanced between two fingers, scar bright in the half-light. The fan turned above, clicking once every third spin.

"You should pack," he said.

"You should run," she said.

"Where."

She didn't answer. Smoke curled and died against the curtain.

Silence grew sharp. Every small sound was amplified, the scrape of her slipper, the whistle of a pressure cooker from another floor, the distant bark of a street dog. All reminders of a world that did not care if they lived or fell.

Finally, she put the cigarette out and turned. "You want the truth tonight?"

He lifted his head. "If it exists."

"I called her. I told her the time. I told her the floor. I wanted her to find him there. I wanted her to look in his eyes and see what I saw every day, a lie rehearsed until it became routine."

His jaw tightened. "You built the rail."

"And you left the door," she said. "Don't pretend your ghosts aren't as bloody as mine."

The drawer called to him. He opened it, pulled the slips, placed them on the table. Her handwriting. His handwriting. Names turned into bullets.

"We both signed," he said. "We both pointed. Maybe we should stop talking as if one of us is clean."

She came closer, stood over him. "You want me to admit more?"

"I want you to admit you'd sell me too."

Her smile was tired, bitter. "I already did."

He nodded once. He almost laughed.

It was not love anymore. It was recognition. They were mirrors facing mirrors, infinite reflections of guilt.

Then she leaned down, kissed him. Not gentle. Not forgiving. A collision.

He didn't resist. His hands gripped her waist, almost bruising. She pulled him up from the chair, dragged him toward the bed like a captive.

They undressed fast, not like lovers but like conspirators shedding disguises. Clothes fell sharp, angry. The bed creaked under their weight.

They came together in silence at first, then in sounds that were closer to violence than passion. His hand pressed against her scar; hers pressed against his bruise. They left marks as if branding each other.

Her breath broke against his ear. "If they ask me tomorrow…"

"Don't," he said.

"I will say your name," she finished.

He pulled her harder, hissed, "Then I'll say yours louder."

They moved with the rhythm of confession, of punishment, of two people who no longer cared if they broke each other open.

When it ended, they lay apart, the sheet a wall between them. Sweat cooled. The fan ticked.

Neither spoke. Neither looked.

Then she rolled onto her side. "Did you hide it?"

He turned his head. "What."

"The photograph," she said.

"I burned it," he said.

"You lie poorly," she said.

"And you?" he asked.

She reached to the floor, lifted her bag, pulled out a folded paper. She threw it onto the bed between them.

The photograph. Balcony frame. The wife's hand. Her note beneath. *He is there now.*

"You kept it," he said.

"So did you," she said.

He sat up, bare chest rising and falling. "Why bring it back tonight?"

"Because tomorrow it will not be ours. Tomorrow it belongs to courtrooms, files, strangers. Tonight, for once, it belongs to us."

He touched the photo, then let go. "So what do we do with it?"

"Nothing," she said. "We let it lie between us, like the truth has all along."

They didn't sleep. They kissed again, slower this time, not with hunger but with exhaustion. They touched as if memorizing what they'd soon lose. It wasn't passion.

It wasn't tenderness. It was the ritual of people who knew goodbye was already written.

Near dawn, she whispered, "If I leave first, don't follow."

"If I leave first," he whispered back, "don't wait."

Their breaths tangled. Neither promised obedience.

[Watcher's Note | Day 46]

Subjects engaged in intimacy. Verbal
exchange: mutual confirmation of betrayal.
Shared possession of incriminating
photograph revealed. Emotional state:
resigned, fatalistic.
Assessment: final cohabitation before
separation.

By morning, the light came weak, filtering through curtains stained with smoke. They dressed without speaking. She tied her hair. He buttoned his shirt wrong again. Neither corrected the other.

The photo still lay on the bed, half under the sheet. Neither reached for it.

At the door, she said, "Tonight was the last."

He nodded. "Yes."

But both knew it wasn't a promise. It was a prophecy.

They locked the flat behind them and walked into a city already awake, knowing the next night might be spent apart, or not at all.

32

The Final Betrayal

The watcher struck first.

An envelope slid under their door before dawn. No stamp. No handwriting. Just weight.

She picked it up, shook it once, slit it with her nail. Out spilled a flash drive, cheap plastic, scratched.

He stared at it. "Play it."

She set it on the table. Neither moved.

"You play it," she said.

"You found it," he said.

The fan ticked. The city stirred below. A vegetable cart rattled past, indifferent.

Finally, he slid the drive into his laptop. The screen woke. A folder blinked open by itself.

One file. Last_Angle.mp4

He double-clicked.

Grainy video. Corridor again. Balcony rail again. Not the wife's hand this time. Not her wrist.

This time: his hand.

The frame caught the moment from behind, from a hidden phone propped against a mop bucket. His fingers stretched toward Ananya. Not to save. To push.

The image froze at the instant of contact. The wife in the frame, turned away. Him — frozen, unmistakable, guilty.

The screen went black.

Neither spoke.

Then a text window popped up over the video. One line.

Payment received. Delivery complete.

He pushed the laptop closed so hard the table shook. "It's false," he said.

She laughed once, bitter, quiet. "It's enough."

"You think they'll believe this?"

"They don't need to believe. They need to file."

He stood, paced the room. "It's a splice. He cut frames. He built it."

"Doesn't matter," she said. "It looks real."

He turned, wild-eyed. "And you? You'll use it."

She didn't answer. She lit a cigarette, inhaled, exhaled toward the ceiling.

"Answer me."

She looked at him through smoke. "If it keeps me alive."

The landline rang. He grabbed it, voice breaking. "What do you want?"

The watcher's calm voice. "I want nothing. I already have the story."

"You doctored it."

"I filmed it," the watcher said. "Truth is angles. One angle frees you, another buries you. I decide which sells."

"You'll hand it to them?"

"I already did," the watcher said. "But only one of you can survive it. The other must burn."

The line clicked.

He dropped the receiver. It swung once, slow, like a pendulum marking time.

She ground her cigarette into the ashtray, eyes steady. "He's given us a choice."

"No," he said. "He's given you an exit and me a grave."

"Not if we're smart," she said.

He barked a laugh. "We're past smart. We're down to animals."

They dressed without looking at each other. The station summoned them again. Square-face wanted signatures, clarifications, devices. The flash drive would be there before them.

At the door, he caught her wrist. "If you hand it over, I'm finished."

She met his eyes. "If I don't, I'm finished."

They stood locked, two people who had spent nights together and were now deciding who'd be left to wake alone.

The station was colder than yesterday. The magistrate wasn't there this time. Only Square-face and the braid officer. The flash drive sat on the table in a clear evidence bag.

Square-face tapped it once. "We received this this morning. Anonymous drop."

He slid it into the computer. Played the clip. The push. The freeze. The silence.

Square-face looked at him. "Your hand."

"It's fake," he said.

Square-face looked at her. "You saw."

She hesitated one second too long. "I saw."

The braid officer leaned forward. "Do you confirm this is Subject M?"

Her scar caught the light. "Yes."

The word landed like a blade.

He stared at her. "You…."

Square-face cut him off. "Enough. You will both sign acknowledgements. We proceed tomorrow with the wife and husband. Today you go back. Tonight, you think about what name you want to carry."

He pushed two forms across the table.

She signed. Steady hand.

He signed. Shaking.

Outside, the sun was white, the pavement hot. They walked home in silence. He ahead, she a step behind.

At the flat, he shut the door hard enough to rattle the glass.

"You chose," he said.

"I survived," she said.

"You killed me."

"I saved myself."

He came close, so close their foreheads almost touched. "We could've lied together."

259

Her eyes were flat. "We did. Until it was time to stop."

They collided again that night. Not love. Not even need. A final act of violence shaped like intimacy. Clothes torn, nails digging, teeth biting. Each touch a sentence: I hate you, I want you, I'll bury you.

After, they lay apart, gasping.

"You'll testify," he said.

"You'll deny," she said.

"And the watcher will win."

"He always does."

[Watcher's Note | Day 47]

Video angle delivered: Subject M hand push. Subject F confirmation obtained. Current state: alliance dissolved, intimacy weaponized, survival path singular. Assessment: imminent fracture.

By dawn, the decision was complete. She left the bed first, packed her bag. His toothbrush still leaned against hers. She didn't touch it.

At the door, she looked back once. "This was the last."

He didn't answer.

She closed the door behind her.

The flat held its silence like a wound.

33

Naked City

Dawn came without apology.

The city was already moving, hawkers balancing baskets, men with kettles, milk vans rattling over potholes. Outside, everything pulsed with the casual cruelty of routine. Inside, the flat held the sour smell of smoke, sweat, and a silence that refused to leave.

He sat at the table, head in hands. Her half of the torn photograph lay beside his elbow. He touched it once, then recoiled as if it burned.

The landline rang. Once. Twice. On the third, he picked up.

"You have been erased," the watcher said.

His voice cracked. "She confirmed."

"Yes. Her voice is clean. Yours is dirtied. That is how the city understands truth."

"Why me?"

"Because only one story sells," the watcher said. "And hers is sharper."

The line died.

By nine, a constable slid a polite letter under his door. Appearance required. Eleven a.m. Magistrate chambers. Bring identification.

He folded it, laid it beside the photograph. For a moment he considered burning both. But flames could not eat what already lived in files and drives and copies.

At eleven he sat under the fan that did not cool. The magistrate scanned the file, then looked at him with weary eyes.

"Your hand," he said.

"It was not mine."

"The camera says otherwise."

"The camera lies."

"The woman does not."

He swallowed. "She needed to survive."

The magistrate scribbled, muttered without looking up: "So do we all."

He signed. He did not read. Each signature felt like a nail.

Square-face did not meet his eyes on the way out. That was worse than contempt. It was dismissal. The city declaring: you are no longer interesting.

Sunlight was too bright. He walked home through streets that smelled of frying bread and urine. Faces seemed to stare, though none did.

At the gate, the watchman ignored him. The register stayed closed.

Upstairs, the flat door hung ajar. Inside, absence had begun. Her clothes gone. Her toothbrush gone. Her half of the photograph gone.

Only his remained, curled, unwanted, a confession no one asked for.

That night he sat on the balcony rail. Below, the pavement still carried a faint stain, memory refusing to die. He thought of her scar. Her laugh. Her lies. The watcher's calm voice looping like a second conscience.

Ash drifted into the dark. He leaned forward once, testing gravity. Pulled back. Lit another cigarette. The flat whispered: no exit.

Across the city, she walked under neon still buzzing from the night. Her bag was light. She carried only what she could lift.

The magistrate had released her with a word that meant both freedom and exile: witness.

She passed a bar where strangers pretended not to be. A tea stall where men argued cricket. A billboard promising love without lies. She smiled at that, bitter.

The city was hers now. Not as lover. As accomplice.

[Watcher's Notes| Day 48]

*Subject M: deteriorating, isolated, high
risk of self-destruction.
Subject F: relocated, free under witness
status.
Watcher note: Only survivors matter.
Survivors feed the story.*

By midnight, he was still on the balcony. The city below had changed shifts, vendors replaced by drinkers, couples sneaking, strays fighting over scraps. He leaned forward, then back. Another cigarette. Another reprieve.

She, meanwhile, sat at a new window in a newer flat. Higher up. Safer walls. Smoke curled into the night. The scar caught the moonlight like a silver signature.

She thought of him, but not tenderly. Thought of the watcher, but not fearfully. Thought of herself, mostly, alive, intact, carrying truth rewritten in her favour.

Tomorrow she would go back to work. Sit at a desk. Smile at colleagues who would not ask. Mumbai would fold her back in as if nothing had happened. That was the city's gift: forgetfulness disguised as resilience.

In his room, dawn seeped again. The torn photograph fluttered under the fan. He pressed it flat, almost believing it could be stitched back whole.

Across the hall, unseen, a phone light blinked once, then died. Another file saved, another angle stored. The watcher did not need to stay. The city was full of couples, passwords, scars. He would choose another window tomorrow.

He laughed then. Low. Bitter. Alone. He tore it again, smaller this time, until nothing remained but fragments carried across the floor.

Acknowledgments

This book would not have been possible without the love, patience, and endless encouragement of those who stood by me during the long nights of writing.

Gratitude to the storytellers and literary voices that inspired me, from James M. Cain to Gillian Flynn, and to the Indian cities that pulse with secrets, contradictions, and restless energy, giving the novel its heart.

To my co-authoring partner in imagination, who helped refine this work chapter by chapter, and to the community of readers who keep my words alive, this book is yours as much as mine.

To my family, for believing in me. To my readers, for giving my work life beyond the page.

And to the city, both beautiful and brutal, thank you for your shadows and your silences.

About the Author

B. S. Dara is the author of the bestselling psychological and crime thriller The Insatiable, the contemporary relationship novel *I, You and Pune*, and *The Lady in Room 302*. He writes about love, betrayal, crime and survival with a cinematic intensity rooted in Indian cities and their contradictions. His stories blend psychological depth with gritty realism, drawing readers into intimate, dangerous worlds. Naked City is his latest psychological thriller.

Also by B. S. Dara

The Insatiable

I, You and Pune

The Lady in Room 302

Author website: bsdara-author.com

www.ingramcontent.com/pod-product-compliance
Lightning Source LLC
Chambersburg PA
CBHW022152170626
46807CB00005B/2176